SS
c.1

Michel, Sam
   Under the light.   Knopf, 1991.
   176 p.

     I. Title.

50394534

90-53574/19.00/691

7-91

UNDER THE LIGHT

Under the Light

STORIES BY

Sam Michel

SS
c.1

ALFRED A. KNOPF

NEW YORK   1991

THIS IS A BORZOI BOOK
PUBLISHED BY ALFRED A. KNOPF, INC.

Certain of these stories first appeared in *The Quarterly,*
Cutbank, and *Neon.* Grateful acknowledgment is made
to these magazines—and to the Sierra Arts Foundation
and the Nevada State Council on the Arts for grants
that subsidized the author in the course of his doing this
work.

Library of Congress Cataloging-in-Publication Data

Michel, Sam.
    Under the light : stories / Sam Michel. — 1st ed.
        p.   cm.
    ISBN 0-394-58723-5
    I. Title.
PS3563.I3325U5   1991
813'.54—dc20   90-53574
                                                      CIP

Manufactured in the United States of America
First Edition

JOYLYN

Contents

A round of thanks and a toast to all—to my mother and my father for being my mother and my father; to Julian and Joanna for the years of meals, the lariat, and the bucking chaps; to Larry and Mariana, Katie and Trevor for making the city possible for me; and to Gordon for pulling me out of the sage and teaching me how to speak. — S M

UNDER THE LIGHT

The Beast, Watered

DAN?" she said.

"Yes?" said Harry.

"What're you doing?" said the girl.

"Putting on my shoes," Harry said.

"God," said the girl. "What time is it?"

"Don't know," said Harry. "Two. Maybe three."

The girl raised herself up on her elbow. He saw her watching him as he buttoned his shirt. He saw her hair hanging down all on one side.

"God," she said, and blinked.

He got his shirt tucked in. He stood with his arms hanging at his sides, considering, then bent down to the girl and put his face next to hers. He lifted her hair up into his face. He rubbed her hair against his face. He breathed the girl's hair up into his face. The girl made a sound. He felt the bed heat of the girl from underneath the covers.

"Got to go," he said.

"Okay," said the girl. "Dan?" she said.

"Yes?" said Harry.

"You'll call me?" she said.

"Sure, you bet," said Harry. "First chance I get."

HE WALKED FAST, crossing the tracks, crossing the bridge, trying to get things going. His breath came out in big clouds. His teeth chattered. He hunched his shoulders and kept walking. Along one full block of shop windows he watched himself walk. At the end of the block he turned, went past three doors, and then went into Ryan's.

"Hey, Harry!" said the bartender. "What's shakin?"

"Plenty," said Harry.

He winked and rubbed his hands together. The bartender grinned and shook his head.

"Coors?" said the bartender.

"Nope," said Harry. "Not tonight. Think I better have some of that whiskey you got."

"Comin up," said the bartender.

"And a pack of something," said Harry. "I don't know— something menthol. And matches."

The bartender screwed up his eyes as he poured the Seagram's.

"You don't smoke, do you?" he said.

"Not much," said Harry.

The bartender came over with the cigarettes and Harry took a ten-dollar bill and a keno ticket from his wallet. On the back of the keno ticket there was a telephone number written. Harry studied the curves of the writing. He lit a cigarette. He saw himself in the bar mirror lighting the cigarette. He held the cigarette near his chest and the smoke curled around his shoulder and past the side of his head. He tried a smile in the mirror. But did not like what he saw there. He crumpled the keno ticket in his palm. Then he held the cigarette down near his knees, watching the smoke split itself around his leg. He kept moving the cigarette to different parts of his body, first with this hand, then with that hand, to his lap, to his neck, his face. He did not let go of the keno ticket. He watched himself.

"Hey, Harry," said the bartender, "gonna smoke that thing or not?"

Harry looked at the bartender. He crushed out the cigarette in the ashtray.

"Guess not," he said.

"I don't know about you," said the bartender.

Harry filled his mouth with the whiskey and puffed out his cheeks, rinsing. He moved his tongue over his teeth. Then he put his nose to his shoulders and to his arms. He pulled his shirtfront up to his nose. He raised his knee to his nose. He checked once more in the mirror, then collected his change, left a tip, and kept the keno ticket.

HE TOOK his shoes off in the hall and turned the key to the door. The latch clicked. He held his breath, pushed through the door, then closed it quietly behind him. He had nearly made it to the bathroom.

"Harry, honey? That you?"

He stood where he was.

"Yeah," he said. His voice sounded funny to him. "It's me," he said.

"God," said the woman. "What time is it?"

"I don't know. One, two." He hated his voice. "Not sure."

He emptied his pockets, keeping the keno ticket in his hand, and started taking off his clothes outside the bathroom.

"What've you been doing?" said the woman.

"Oh, you know. Ryan's."

He moved just outside the bedroom door. He could see her in there, propped on her elbow.

"Coming to bed?" she said.

"No," he said. "Not unless you want to sleep with a saloon. Think I'll get a shower. Pretty smoky in that place. Check these."

He tossed his trousers and his shirt onto the bed and turned to go to the bathroom.

IN THE BATHROOM, he took one more look at himself, then squeezed the keno ticket into a tiny ball. He got on his knees and dug through the bag under the sink. He dug through tampons, through disposable razors, through hair, and through wads of Kleenex before sticking the keno ticket down at the bottom.

He shaved twice.

He urinated—and he noticed the smell!

It smelled to him as if he had been eating something funny. He stood there at the toilet awhile before flushing it.

He turned on the shower and got the water very hot, and waited in front of the mirror until the glass fogged.

The Beast, Watered

He stepped into the shower, bent his neck, and let the water wash down over his head. He tried not to think—not about the funny smell or about the keno ticket or the cigarettes or the girl's hair. He let the water wash down over his head until he no longer needed to try not to think. Then he raised his head and let the water hit him in the chest.

He got out of the shower. But he did not get a towel. Instead, he dropped to his knees, pulled the bag from under the sink again, and began going through the tampons, the hair, the Kleenex, the shit. He felt his heart beating. His ears filled with the sound of his heart beating. He dumped the bag on the floor and spread the stuff out, his eyes moving over everything, his fingers testing everything. He tried to remember the girl's face. He tried to remember her voice. He tried to remember anything she had said or what she had felt like when he had felt her. But there was only the funny smell.

He kept pawing on his knees.

Seeing Hunter Creek

Pete's arm! Sixty-two years old, that arm was. Looking at it, Harry could not believe it, but it was, was sixty-two, and the rest of Pete, too—both legs, chest, liver, heart, the high-held shoulder from where that sided arm used to hang—all of it, Harry knew: sixty-two.

To see it work! To see that arm hammer and lift and dig! To see it—from Harry's fifteen-year-old's shoes—not shrivel and scale, but grow and shine: humping lumber, digging ditches, clearing scrap, doing the kind of work that sent high school and college students—even Mexicans—packing. To see it work the knife and cut the meat, shuffle up and deal the deck. To see it touch a woman's back! To see Pete's arm now, suddenly, after a lifetime, with re-memberings of it, wonderings on it, expectations for it, was a thing as to fill Harry with fear and joy and hope.

It was a thing, to see Pete's arm reaching, then lifting, then standing those walls—how many walls?—that made Harry's heart rise to his throat and, if nobody was watching, pump his fist high in the air. It was the arm, in Harry's mind, at that time, the rope-muscled and dove-tattooed arm, that made Pete, made what he said true, or if not true, then at least believable, and if not that, then the arm, hammer-sharp pounding out punctuation to some story big and wild, made Harry want to forget what was and was not true, and for the time of Pete's speaking, believe in a world he, Harry, would wish could be.

"WATCH OUT!" Harry shouted. "Watch him now! Give him room," he said. "He's got to have *breathing* room."

Harry had six takers on the bet, the bet to see whether if Pete could lift Harry's father's diesel Mercedes—it had taken four of the boys to do it—dollar a wager. Harry had positioned one of the takers on each side of the car, to help keep the balance.

"You didn't say he was going to need help," said one of the boys.

"I said he'd lift the damn thing," said Harry, "and he will. If you want to see him balance it," he said, "it'll cost you another buck."

The boys were quiet then as Pete settled into a squat at the business end of the car. Harry shifted his eyes back and forth from the boys to Pete, who was staring hard now at the bumper, a single shining spot on the bumper, and nothing else but that spot. Pete laid his hand on that spot, stroked it. He worked his hand, clenching and stretching his fingers, before sliding his hand under the bumper, and with set jaw, but no sound—no grunts, no air from his nose, none of it—Pete lifted, straight-backed, coming steadily out of the squat.

Nobody said a word until Pete reached his full height and stopped lifting, the Mercedes balanced, on the one hand, and with no help. Then the same boy who had spoken earlier said, "All's he used was his legs; you told us he'd do it with his arm," and Harry saw something change in Pete's eyes, and Pete began to do it: skin stretching tighter over his biceps, veins standing out on his forearm, the car rose higher, was raised to Pete's waist, balancing, never wavering, the boys standing on each side with their hands held up and their mouths slacked wide, Pete grinning, lowering the car back to the pavement; and as Harry watched, he recognized in Pete's eyes the same change he'd seen in the rodeo bull's eyes, when the animal has thrown the man, and has sighted him on his knees, scrambling to find his feet.

THEY WERE SITTING in Pete's place, Harry and Pete, sipping Pete's medicine. It was a Sunday afternoon, hot. They had quit with the cards because of the heat and were taking turns looking through the telescope. Neither wore a shirt. Harry kept trying not to look at the scar-slicked purple of Pete's stump, tried watching instead the sweat beads rolling off the chilled bottle, Pete's hand gripping the neck. Harry was waiting for Pete to go back to the telescope, so he could get another shot at that bottle.

What Pete was saying, was how in this town, in his time, Pete's time, back when he had two arms, a guy could do anything whatever it was he wanted to do. Anything! he was saying. All of it! *Imagine it.* Say a guy wanted to fish, or get divorced quick. He could do that. Both of that.

Divorce, sure, shit. But try to fish now, he was saying, and see what you pull out of that creek. Try to hunt. Look across this valley in winter, tell me what you see. We didn't know what a *temperature inversion* was, he was saying, because we'd never been able to see one! And the water, the water! Would you drink from a public swimming pool? There were ladies then, too, like there aren't ladies now. Ask one of the ladies down at the house to do you straight up—straight up!—for a Lincoln spot. And disease! You'd better double-bag it now, boy, because you'll catch yourself something a whole lot worse than the clap to brag on. For laughs, he was saying, try this: try stretching naked in the morning sun on your porch, your own damn back porch! Or say a man, a waiter, say, is rude, to your wife, say. Poke him in the nose, why don't you? Gather up his collar, poke him! See how many people you know down at the clubs, how many remember that that's your seat, by God, your lucky-for-blackjack seat, and see if a stranger will switch you when you tell him so. Tell me how many people you know who are from here, or have a head to stay here, or give a rat's ass about what's going on here? In his time, Pete was saying, a person couldn't beat this place for land or town or people.

"It's no good," said Pete, "when a thing's too good."

Pete raised his bottle, and Harry watched the swallow Pete's throat made. Pete set the bottle down, scratched at his stump, turned back to the telescope. Pete was focusing, Harry knew—his fingers so light on the dials—far up the mountain, focusing on a place even the power of the scope could not find from where they stood, a place Pete had told Harry about, the best Pete had ever built, but Harry

—despite the number of times he'd been up there—had never yet seen, deep in the fir and pine tree forest, near an aspen stand, near Hunter Lake, a place Pete had built under the cool shade there, and kept secret.

PETE GOT HIMSELF twenty-eight stitches over his right eye. Three bones broken in his hand, he got, and his middle finger. One hundred and thirty-six stitches ran from the inside of his elbow, up across the dove tattoo, clear to the outside of his shoulder. The finger, Pete figured, came when he put his hand through the refrigerator case. The hand and the arm, he said, came from the front door that didn't give, and didn't give, then finally gave. His eye, Pete explained, came from the security guard and the clerk, who knocked him down, the counter corner catching him just there, just right.

"Why?" Harry asked.

"Because the guy couldn't speak English," said Pete. "Because the guy wouldn't change a hundred-dollar bill," he said. "Because," he said, "there was no*body* there. Because," Pete said, "if you are going to say something worth saying, you'd better make sure somebody hears it."

THEY LOOKED to Harry like dinosaurs; monstrous, prehistoric things. They always had. Big, belching, ripping, roaring yellow things. Metal and rubber, oil and gas. Bucket-bellied and saber-toothed: this one tearing, that one hauling, the other dumping—one to digest, even, sucking up and spewing out, and another rolling around and around, pissing down the flying dust.

Harry stood next to Pete, watching the brush and curve of Hunter Creek hill flatten out and blow away. Harry was Pete's help now—now that Pete's hand and arm were the way they were—his assistant, his boy.

ON BREAK, at the burger joint, Harry watched Pete trying to eat, how slow it went for Pete. Harry ate his own fast, and had already started in on the second bag of fries, when things began dropping from Pete's hand. First a bit of onion. A pickle. Some mustard and ketchup. Then it happened that the whole thing split itself in half, just at Pete's mouth, and Harry saw the way Pete's other side, the no-armed side, moved—like to catch it.

They sat staring that way, at the mess there in the Styrofoam box, Pete's hand resting next to it—the cast, the splint. Nobody moved a thing an inch, and the music in that time seemed loud to Harry. Finally, something like a smile, Harry saw, came to Pete's lips, and Harry watched as Pete fished around in the paper sack, began lining out the little packets of ketchup and mayonnaise on the table.

Harry gave a jerk, and winced to see it, when Pete's fist came down on the first packet, and then the second, the third, the fourth, the stuff splattering everywhere.

"Senators!" Pete was shouting. "Infidelity! Japs and water meters! California!" he shouted. "New fucking York!"

. . .

"KILL THOSE LIGHTS," Pete said.

Harry switched off the pickup lights and the flat site went black. He rolled down his window, heard off in the brush the whine and buzz of the nighttime insects. Harry heard Pete loading shells.

Pete was saying, "I've been building all my life. I've built the best places in this town," he said. Pete said, "I've pulled enough sliver wood from my body to frame a whole house."

Harry watched Pete working the chamber, the .12 gauge pinched between his knees. Pete swigged from the medicine bottle, making the liquid-in-glass sound, and handed the bottle to Harry and got out of the pickup. Harry did not turn his head, but could feel Pete looking him over there through the open window. Harry could feel the shotgun barrel resting against the pickup door.

Pete said, "You're all right, boy? You know what to do?"

"Sure, I know," said Harry, and kept staring out, his palms wet on the wheel, trying not to think how it would look in the morning, in the light.

Pete said, "This town, boy, is hellbent for mediocrity."

TO THE EAST, across the valley and behind the mountains, Harry saw the first tip of the rising moon. He saw the yellow come back into the dark shapes of the tractors and trucks, and the alkali white of the laser-leveled, tractor-graded earth. By daylight, it had not seemed so big to

Harry, but as the moon rose to quarter view, half, then full—the flat, luminous area appeared greater than five, ten, fifteen football fields, all pushed together, a giant stadium glowing under the bright reflected light, edged around by the tangled hedge of sage and bitter brush, wild peach, wild rose. It felt funny to Harry, seeing Hunter Creek hill stripped that way, and it made the hair stand up on his arms, as if he had seen a ghost, or a car-struck dog, not quite dead, never coming back.

Above himself Harry heard Pete's hand, tap-tapping on the pickup roof. From the brush he heard the dove's coo, the owl's hoot. From up the hill he could hear the down-spilling rush of Hunter Creek, making its way to the ditch below where Harry could hear the leaves of the cotton-wood blowing brittle.

Then, from everywhere Harry looked, creeping in from around the perimeter, as if by signal, or else by magic— the rabbits. Rabbits moving two, three hops, crawling, almost, then stopping, raising noses, cocking ears, testing the air, then moving again toward the center of the clearing. Big and small, jack and cottontail, waves of rabbits, hundreds of rabbits, it seemed to Harry, moving toward the center, toward the open.

At Harry's ear, Pete said, he whispered, "Ready?" and Harry hit the brights, and the rabbits froze.

PETE STOPPED WALKING, asked Harry what time it was.

"About seven," said Harry.

Pete looked up at the sky, then east, down the tracks. Harry did the same, seeing the twin lines converging in the distance, the buildings—casinos and restaurants—rain-washed and sharp, and the clouds, already past them, headed for Utah and Idaho and beyond, still raining down, he saw, and colored the desert colors of sunset. Harry breathed deep, smelled the wet gravel and the pavement, felt the end-of-summer air, felt the sharp beginning of things changing.

It had been a good summer, and the building had gone well, it being hard already for Harry to tell what Hunter Creek hill had once looked like, hard even to remember, hard to care. Even Pete, Harry thought, seemed caught up in the fast-moving sweep of work. Harry looked at Pete—Pete's arm, the sun-leathered lines in his sixty-two-year-old face.

Pete said, "We'll go this way."

They walked along the tracks, on Commercial Street, and Harry felt great, his first one-hundred-dollar bill aflame in his pocket. They had been to cash their checks at the club, and Pete had loaned Harry five bucks to put on top of his ninety-five-dollar earnings, to let Harry get the big bill. Pete turned, leaving the street, and walked through the gravel, right up to the tracks. He knelt down in the gravel, put his hand on the rail. Then Pete stood up and asked Harry for a nickel. Harry gave Pete the nickel. Pete laid the nickel on the rail where his hand had been, took two steps back.

"Put your hand on that rail, boy," Pete said. "What do you feel?"

"It tickles," said Harry. "Feels like tickling."

When the train had passed, clacking and wranging and banging by two steps close—Harry had never stood so close—Pete had Harry go and find the nickel: flat, distorted, some old President's face—Jefferson's, Harry thought—a metal smear.

"That's it," Pete said, and wiggled the shoulder on the no-armed side. "Right here in this place. Right there on that spot," said Pete. "That's how I lost her."

HARRY DIDN'T LIKE the weight of the tool bags hanging on his hips—the way they pulled his pants down, the impressions left on his skin—and he took them off, generally, when he did not need to use the things in them. He was standing on the roof, stacking sheets of plywood that Pete was sliding up to him on the two-by-four ramp—three-quarter-inch sheets, four feet by ten, sixty-two years old!—when Harry stopped to unclip the belt.

Pete said, "You leave those things on, boy."

"Why?" said Harry.

"Why," Pete said, "because they're lifesavers; that's why."

"Lifesavers?" Harry said.

"Your hammer," said Pete, "is your best friend in high places. Your hammer and your arm," Pete said.

Pete began to climb the ladder, one-arming his way up the rungs. Up top, next to Harry, Pete gathered together a fistful of sawdust, threw the sawdust all over a spot on the steep-sloped roof.

"Hold my hand," Pete said, "and you just go on ahead and put your foot out on that dust."

Harry did what Pete said, felt his feet begin to slide. He felt Pete's grip holding him back. Then, without a word between them, Harry saw Pete, Pete's hammer in his hand, his arm cocked out from his side—on the ready—step out onto the dust. Harry watched Pete slide, knees bent, to the edge, where Pete jumped, out and away from the house, and spun—in midair—his big arm holding the hammer high above his head, then bringing it down, claw side first, fast, and hard, the claw striking, but not sticking—the way Harry knew Pete thought it would—but bouncing: the arm, the hand, the hammer, everything going down, over the edge, and out of Harry's sight.

Harry went to the edge, saw Pete there on the ground, flat on his back. He could see Pete's mouth opening and closing, trying to get the air in, trying to get back all that had gone out. Harry could see Pete's eyes—wide and wild, finally afraid.

SNOW HAD FALLEN in the night. Harry woke up and looked out on it, a thin-skinned layer of it, the season's first, lying white and silent, just outside the little lodgepole lean-to, way up on the mountain, in the secret place Pete had built, not a stone's throw from Hunter Lake. Harry had found the place easily—Pete had told about it so much before he had moved away. Harry could not believe he had never seen the place before, could not believe much of all of what he saw while seeing so high up, seeing for the very first time now something new in everything old.

Harry reached and touched one of the poles, touched the manzanita woven tight between the poles: so tight that no wind came in from the sides, so tight that neither rain nor snow nor anything would come down in from above.

Seeing Hunter Creek

Harry left the lodgepole lean-to, crossed through the woods—the firs, the clean, pine scent—his steps making no sound in the new-fallen snow. He made his way to the lake, and once there was surprised to see how from where he stood the town was out of sight, just as this place had been out of sight from the telescope in town. Harry skirted the lake—the green reeds, the snow-crowned cattails—to where the lake became a creek, Hunter Creek, that flowed down out of these woods and manzanita, through the sage and bitter brush, the wild peach and rose, on past the ravine and into the ditch below Hunter Creek hill. He followed the creek awhile, then turned off into the aspen grove— white-barked, quaking, yellow leaves against a cobalt sky. Harry began reading things etched into the bark of the aspen: names, promises, obscenities. JIM and LARRY, he read. SARAH 1982. KEN LOVES LAURIE. FUCK YOU and EAT SHIT. Harry kept walking, deeper into the grove, until he felt he must be in the center of it, and there was nothing he could see but the trunks and limbs and leaves and sky, lost in it, looking, now, on his own in it, and there, on what Harry guessed must have been the biggest tree of all, high up on the trunk, right where Pete said it would be, almost too high up to read, was carved PETE 1943, plain and bold, still alive, and growing.

Smoke

THE TIMMONSES stood facing Harry on Harry's porch. Harry stood in his doorway. He was wishing he hadn't answered their knock without his shirt. It felt funny to him, standing there without a shirt. He thought maybe Mr. Timmons felt the same way. There was a look in Mr. Timmons's eye. It really was funny—because Harry and the Timmonses had never met.

"We're the Timmonses," Mrs. Timmons said, and then one thing led to another until she was holding Mr. Timmons's elbow and saying, "Well, then, just don't call it a divorce ranch, honey."

"What else do you expect me to call it?" said Mr. Timmons, "when that's what it is? Do you expect if I call it something else it'll be different, or what? It seems funny, is all, a divorce ranch. I hope it's worth it to you, living out here."

"Oh, it is," said Mrs. Timmons. "It's lovely out here."

Harry kept his arms folded over his chest and tried not

looking at the Timmonses, who had just moved into the cottage across the courtyard, number three. Separated by the clothesline and the little stretch of lawn, number three was no different from Harry's cottage. Harry knew that because he had snuck through number three when the last people had moved out. It was just like his was, only empty. He had wondered who would move in and what kind of things they would have and whether they would be the kind of people who have plants. And now here they were, on his porch, the Timmonses.

Harry figured he already knew some things about the Timmonses. He had watched them from his window as they hauled in boxes, tables, chairs from the U-Haul. It looked to him the way it always looked, the moving and the stuff being moved. It was young stuff. First-marriage stuff. Harry knew which of the stuff was Mr. Timmons's and which was Mrs. Timmons's. He knew they would have to take the bed apart to get it through the door. What he didn't know was whether the Timmonses were the kind of people to go and get plants.

Harry had thought about helping.

He scratched his chest and felt his navel for lint.

"Don't you think so, Drake?" Mr. Timmons was saying.

"What?" said Harry.

"Don't you think it's funny, living on an old divorce ranch?" Mr. Timmons said.

Harry hooked his thumbs in his pockets and stared at his naked feet.

. . .

THAT WAS in April.

Mrs. Timmons started doing Harry's wash in May. It was after the time a pair of red socks turned his white things pink. She caught him in the laundry room holding up his sheet to the light, and when he told her no, these sheets were not supposed to be pink, Mrs. Timmons said, "I'll tell you what, how would you like for me to do your wash? Really," said Mrs. Timmons. "It's no trouble. It's part of why I, we, moved out here. I never really got a sense of neighbors, living there in town. Honest, it's no trouble. You work," she said. "You're a bachelor. You could probably do me a favor someday. I wash Mondays."

Mrs. Timmons took the sheet from Harry.

"Besides," she said, "I just can't see a fella like you sleeping on pink."

IN JULY, it began hitting over a hundred out and Harry lost his job. At first it wasn't so bad. He kept busy with unemployment papers, television, bologna logs, and five-pound bricks of government cheddar. He slept until noon and carried the fan with him wherever he went—bathroom, living room, kitchen. There was no reason to go out, and he didn't.

"This is the life," he said to himself. "Beats hell out of banging nails."

He thought he could go on eating bologna, cheddar, and ketchup sandwiches forever, and there was a little girl on *Days of Our Lives* he lived to see get corked. Every day he woke up, carried the fan into the living room, rubbed his hands together, and said, "See if she gets corked today."

He was surprised at the way he felt. He took it personally. She was a tease. Harry thought about it. A tease. He felt he knew a tease when he saw one.

HE SAT STILL on the sofa watching. The fan air moved his hair. His stomach begged for bologna and cheddar. But only the sound of a tire iron outside got him up.

He saw Mrs. Timmons changing a flat tire. But he heard his stomach, and went to the kitchen to make a sandwich.

He spent the day and the night watching television in front of the fan. He thought he might be getting a stomach-ache. He blamed the bologna. Too much of a good thing. Maybe tomorrow, he thought, he could doctor it with Top Ramen.

He switched off the television, dragged his fan to the bathroom, washed his armpits, brushed his teeth.

It was then he learned, if he put his ear to it, he could hear what the Timmonses were saying from number three.

"Poor man, my ass!" he heard Mr. Timmons yelling. "The lousy son-of-a-bitch doesn't work! Hell with that neighbor garbage! He can do his own wash!"

Harry turned off the fan. There was a waiting sort of no sound for a while and then he heard Mrs. Timmons say, "Well, he changed a tire for me today."

Sweat beaded on Harry's forehead.

NEXT DAY Harry cleaned house. He dragged the fan into the kitchen and started in with the vacuum. He vacuumed over the open part of the floor twice. He moved the table

and chairs and vacuumed until the foot impressions were
sucked up flat. With the nozzle attachment he vacuumed
in the space between the stove and the cupboards, vacuumed cobwebs out of corners, vacuumed dust and dead
flies from windowsills. He moved the fan into the bathroom, then into the bedroom, vacuuming around the mirror, along the base of the tub, under the bed, behind the
dresser. He filled an entire bag and then he was finished.
He threw the bag away, closed his eyes, and put his face
up close to the fan on the kitchen table.

It was surprising to him what he had been living with.

He opened the refrigerator and pulled out the bologna
and the cheddar. Then he remembered his stomach. He
turned on the television. But it was Saturday and there was
nothing on he really wanted to watch.

He decided to shave and take a shower.

He shaved carefully, making sure to catch even the whiskers under his nose and on his neck. He splashed water
on his face and checked closely, seeing how the fan moved
the soapy water across his chin. Then he stepped into the
shower. He soaped, scrubbed, rinsed, and did it all again.
Behind his ears, in his ass, the bottoms of his feet. He
washed his hair. The water felt good. He tried touching
his toes. He straightened up and reached his hands to the
ceiling. He parted the curtains, wiped the water from the
window, saw Mr. Timmons across the courtyard lighting
a barbecue.

Mrs. Timmons stood behind Mr. Timmons. Harry saw
her look up and see him in the window. He was almost
sure of it. He saw goose pimples on his arms and legs. He

shuddered when he moved closer to the fan and rolled the Speed Stick under his arms. The mirror told him he was ready. He could never be readier.

"I'm ready," he said, and the sound of his voice startled him. He said it again, his lips right up against the fan. "I'm ready," he said.

THE SMELL of chicken teriyaki made its way across the courtyard and through his window and mixed in the fan air with the smell of shrimp Ramen. Harry cut a thick slab off the cold bologna log and slapped it into a frying pan. The bologna spat and sizzled in the pan and when the singed edges curled, Harry forked the meat and flipped it over. The bologna was quiet until he pressed down where the center stood up from the pan. When it was just right, he forked the meat onto a plate and poured the Ramen on it. He carried the plate to the table, and then dragged the fan over. He fetched a napkin from the cupboard and a knife from the drawer. He checked his window. Mrs. Timmons was there, under her porch light, holding the plate of chicken teriyaki. He didn't see her go back into her place, but saw her standing there, looking at his door.

Harry moved from the window. He held his breath. Then he hurried, clearing pots and pans from the stove, his plate from the table, putting everything into the refrigerator. He unplugged the fan, carried it to the living room, and sat on the sofa and waited. He waited until he decided she was not going to come.

He carried the fan back into the kitchen and opened the

refrigerator and saw the Ramen and bologna under the bright bulb. It hadn't seemed so gray. He stuck his finger in it.

Brick cold.

He left it there and closed the refrigerator.

HE HEARD LAUGHTER, her laughter, Mrs. Timmons's laughter. He switched the fan to low and he heard through Mrs. Timmons's laughter Mr. Timmons's voice.

Harry pulled a chair up to the window. He listened awhile and then he turned off all his lights.

He could see their shapes. He saw them at their table behind the window shade. He watched. He saw her feed him with her hand. He saw Timmons shake his head and heard him growl like a dog. He heard Mrs. Timmons laugh again, saw her throw up her hands, lean back in her chair while Mr. Timmons raised a glass to his lips. Mrs. Timmons stood and reached a glass out to Mr. Timmons.

He saw Mrs. Timmons's shape go away.

Nothing happened for a time except some talking Harry couldn't hear through the fan. He tried switching the fan off, but it got too hot. Mr. Timmons might be smoking, Harry thought.

Finally, he saw her come back again.

Then the kitchen light went out.

Harry put his elbows on his knees and his forehead in his hands. He closed his eyes, opened them, then closed them again. He straightened up and filled his lungs with air. He tilted his head back and let the air out.

His chest ached.

He saw the bathroom light come on.

Then the bedroom.

He took the fan into his bedroom, switched it on high, and took his clothes off. On his knees, on his bed, he watched.

A shape appeared behind the bedroom shade—Mrs. Timmons's.

Harry leaned forward, his hands on the windowsill. The shade went up, and there was Mrs. Timmons getting her blouse off.

Then the bathroom light went off and the window shade came down.

It got quiet.

Harry leaned forward again, put his ear to the screen. He shut the fan off.

He stood up on his bed, trying to get a better angle, but it was like trying to look up a skirt on TV.

He suddenly thought he heard Mr. Timmons say "Honey." Harry thought he heard Mr. Timmons say that—say "Honey."

He jerked off. He wiped it off with his sheet. He turned on the fan.

THERE WAS NOTHING left to vacuum. He didn't need a shave. He kept an eye out over the clothesline and the lawn and he listened. He thought he would maybe put out his eyes and ears, or move into town.

When Monday morning came, Harry found himself in bed, peering out his window while Mr. Timmons started his car and left for work. Harry got up, pissed, carried the fan to the living room. He watched the morning news, learned the high would be 105, thought how bad the plans you make late at night seem by the light of day.

All in all, he felt pretty good.

He made a new plan.

First, he got his dirty clothes, towels, sheets, into the laundry basket. Next, he wrote a note saying he was sick and could Mrs. Timmons please just take these things and leave them when she was finished. He set the basket and the note on his porch, stared out his window, then closed all the curtains and turned the volume up on the TV.

Then he climbed out of the sofa to go find something to eat. He carried the fan to the kitchen and began searching the cupboards. He found lime Jell-O.

"Okay," he said.

He mixed the Jell-O and put it in the refrigerator and unplugged the fan. He started for the living room, then went to look through the curtain to check on his laundry. The basket was gone.

The game shows were on. Then it was time for *Days of Our Lives*. He watched awhile, then hurried to inspect the Jell-O. He put his finger in it. He heard Mrs. Timmons in the courtyard. He closed the refrigerator. He parted the curtains over the sink. She was out there, wearing a bathing suit, hanging the wash to dry. Harry noticed the way the elastic crept up her buttocks when she reached to hang something. He saw there was nothing so wonderful about her body.

He went back.

The boyfriend had his hands on her shoulders. The girl was telling him she didn't know, she wasn't sure, didn't think she was old enough, didn't think it was right. Did he love her? If he loved her, he would understand.

"Understand, shit," said Harry, "poor guy just wants a shot at the bearded clam."

He turned off the TV, carried the fan to the kitchen, parted the curtains over the sink. Harry saw how Mrs. Timmons hadn't done anything about her elastic, how it had crept up even farther. He saw how she was halfway through hanging things. He let the curtains fall back, took the Jell-O from the refrigerator, a knife from the drawer. He cut a square in the Jell-O and tried lifting it with the knife. The Jell-O spread all around the knife. The knife did not lift anything up.

He tried a spoon. He gave it up and went to get his mirror sunglasses.

THE HEAT OUTSIDE went into his lungs. Even the sunglasses could not cut the glare. He steadied himself on the porch railing.

"Holy smokes," he said.

Mrs. Timmons turned at his voice. She smiled. He saw that there were spots on the suit below her breasts and at her navel.

"Feeling better?" she said.

"Little," Harry said.

"Summer cold?" she said.

"Stomach thing," Harry said.

She did not fix her elastic.

"Flu?" she said. "My husband says there's a bug going around town."

Harry left his porch, went toward her.

"No," Harry said. "Think it might be bologna. Been eating a lot of bologna."

"Bologna?" said Mrs. Timmons. "Is that all you eat?"

"That and cheddar. Bologna and cheddar. And Top Ramen. You can doctor it up some with Top Ramen and it's okay," Harry said.

Mrs. Timmons kept squeezing a clothespin open and shut.

"Sounds awful," she said. "Bologna. A man can't live on bologna and Ramen. You better have lunch with me. Leftover chicken. We barbecued it the other night, teriyaki. Pretty good."

Harry didn't say anything. Mrs. Timmons turned back to the clothesline. The elastic had crept halfway up. He thought how that must feel.

"You want a hand?" he said.

"Well, sure," Mrs. Timmons said. "Pins are in that coffee can. You just go help yourself."

He grabbed a handful of clothespins. He took a towel and a shirt. He picked up a pair of his pants. Sweat stung his eyes and blurred his vision. He blinked, and it was when he blinked that the clothespin snapped closed, catching the loose part of some skin just right.

He dropped the pants, shook his finger, said, "Sonofabitch!"

"Oh," said Mrs. Timmons, "you all right?"

Harry took his finger from his mouth. There was a blood blister there.

"Boy, that smarts," he said.

Mrs. Timmons came close, put her hands on either side

of his hand, but did not touch his hand. She pouted and looked into Harry's sunglasses.

"Let me hang these last few things," she said, "and then I'll take you into the house and see if we can't make it feel a little better."

HARRY DID NOT take off the sunglasses inside. He left them on and through them he saw everything he had already seen when they had moved in. The table, the chairs, the lamp with the lace frills. The clock set in lacquered redwood hung on the wall, and the free-standing bookcase held the unboxed photographs, pots, pans.

Mrs. Timmons bent to take the chicken teriyaki from the refrigerator. Harry watched her bend. She put the stuff on the table. She looked Harry's way, then dumped the ashtray in the garbage under the sink and said, "Disgusting habit he has. Do you smoke?"

"Sometimes," said Harry.

"Drink?"

"Not now."

"Come on back to the bedroom," she said. "I've got some needles there that should do the trick for that blister."

"Needles?" said Harry.

"To relieve the pressure," said Mrs. Timmons.

Harry followed her. He followed her through the living room, past the bathroom, into the bedroom. He felt the difference, seeing the rooms and the furniture in the rooms, now that they were together and the people used them.

"I usually just leave them be," he said.

"Don't be silly," she said.

In the bedroom, standing at the foot of the bed, he looked from their window across the courtyard to the closed curtained reflection of his own windows. He watched Mrs. Timmons searching drawers for a needle to relieve the pressure.

"Voilà!" she said, and straightened up, looking, Harry thought, right through his sunglasses.

"Will it be safe?" Harry said.

"Safe?" said Mrs. Timmons.

"I mean, will I get an infection?"

"Oh, I doubt it," said Mrs. Timmons. "But I'll sterilize it if you like."

Harry saw her pick up a lighter from the top of the bureau and hold the flame to the needle. He wiped the sweat from his forehead with the back of his arm.

"You'll be careful?" he said.

"Of course," she said. "Don't be such a baby. Now," she said, and reached for Harry's hand.

"Just be careful," he said.

She took his hand in hers, trying to steady his finger. She touched the needle to the purple blister. Harry thought he could see his pulse in the blister.

"Relax," she said.

Harry took a deep breath and held it. He turned his head from his finger. He looked again at the bed and again out the window and then he said, "Did you see me in the shower?"

"Yes," she said.

She stuck him.

She stuck him and he flinched and the needle drove into the meat of his finger. Blood spread out from the blister.

He tried to pull his hand back. He felt himself trying to pull his hand back.

But she would not let go.

She held him.

"There's more," she said, and stuck him again.

Under the Light

IT WAS a bone cracker for sure, the last fastball that caught her just below the elbow bone. Too bad she ducked. Too bad she turned her head and blinked. Too bad for her, Harry said, she didn't hang in there and catch it. If he and Tom had told her once, then they'd told her over a hundred billion times before to watch the ball and use the mitt, and not just only the mitt's middle part either, but the webbed part mostly, if ever anyway she wanted those purple welts of broken vessels in her hand to heal. No use, Harry said, for her to bellyache and ask to pitch. She had had her chance and was strictly minor league. This was the majors. Sliders, curves, and knucklers, split fingers and spitters—stuff she didn't have. If she wanted to play—and she was lucky, really, they let her play, Harry said—she had to catch. Too bad, he said, he was sorry, Harry told his mother, that she always, always, always bailed out, turned her head and blinked exactly when she oughtn't.

But, still, "Oh, man!" Harry said to Tom, "did you hear that smack? I mean, like my dad's leather belt, that smack was. It was rocks against concrete! Take a look," Harry said, and lifted up his mother's glove-sided arm from off where it was lying limp against his mother's body lying on its side like to sleep. "Did you ever see a thing like this? Stitches? Stitches?" Harry said, touching his finger to where the ball's lacing had made an imprint on the slack-skinned place which was closer really, Harry noticed, a red and swelling stamp of cross-hatched baseball stitching, really closer to the more breakable part of his mother's blue-veined wrist than to her elbow.

Harry and Tom took a side each in heaving Harry's mother up from where she was down to finish off the full count. Harry walked back and forth in front of his mother, holding his one arm slung low from the shoulder, showing her how to shake it out. Three balls and two strikes was the count, Harry was telling his mother, two outs, bottom of the ninth, bases loaded. No time for pain-complaining sissy-wristers. The game?—Bottom of the ninth, 1963. No chokes! "One more man," he told her. "We've got to get this one last man!"

Harry's mother socked her fist into his father's mitt. She palm-jostled her crotch like a major leaguer. She rubbed spit into the stitched-in stamp above her wrist. She squatted onto her haunches and showed to Harry the sweet spot for the final strike.

What a sport!

What a mother!

Every pitch—bottom of the ninth, 1963!—every pitch always the last pitch! No chokes, no way! They were hot! They were on! Never did they not get their last man. Nearly every day of most of that summer they had lost some men

but never at least in their game the last man. In the in-
between evening and nighttime time of barbecue breezes
searing over neighborhood fences there were windups and
pitches and strikeouts that left Harry, his mother, and Tom
the high-fiving champions of the backyard world they, the
all of them, lived together in.

What else? Champagne is what else! What else but champagne? Champagne and orange juice for the champs! Mimosas, Harry's mother said, no more than two apiece for
Harry and Tom, please, she said, Harry's mother popping
off the cork top for Harry and Tom to fight to catch,
Harry's mother next flopping down to soak whatever part
of herself she had used that day instead of the mitt in the
ice chest the champagne all summer long chilled in, Harry's
mother having soaked so far this summer her foot, her
shin, her knee, her other foot, her cheek, and now today
her elbow, or not her elbow but the still—even still!—lace-
stamped place nearer to her wrist. T-bones, too, is what
else! Harry aimed his nose at the side neighbor's slump-
stone wall and used a summer's worth of smelling to pick
out burning beef from what tonight was neither chicken,
lamb, nor pork and began to chant T-bone! T-bone!
T-BONE! with Tom joining in and with Harry's mother
downing her mimosa and hauling herself up and out to
the garage and the meat-locker deep freeze to fetch her
boys some sixteen-ouncers. Burgers and dogs, fries, chips,
and pickles, biting tomatoes like apples—and skip the chin
napkins—rolling corn on the cob straight in the butter,
eating fancy olives one by one from off of each finger, nor
either to forget the nose-fuzzing mimosas, and the sweet
things, too, cakes, cookies, pies, and ice cream, homemade,

hand-cranked and rock-salted, June 11, July 19, August 28, none of them the days of birthdays or holidays of anybody or of anything any of them knew about or cared about except to celebrate the every day that they were the champs, that they had got the one last man, full count, bases loaded, had struck him out, bottom of the ninth, 1963!

Harry and Tom sat and sipped their mimosas, resting up for the night game of what would mark their first doubleheader, both of them waiting on the dark to try out the light, each of them forearm deep now in his own bag of the brand-name, good kind of ridged-type dippers—no more jippo bargain chips for champs!

"What a life!" Harry said.

"Can you beat it?" Tom said.

"Sure you can beat it!" Harry said.

You could beat it with a real catcher, Harry said, who never bailed out, one who you could throw as hard as you could at and not have to feel bad about it after. Or good about it. Because even though you could never tell it to your mother, it did feel pretty good, Harry said, tagging her that way without really having even to try too hard, and so much feeling good over a mean thing like that could always make a person feel pretty bad about himself. There was that for sure—the feeling good when you ought to feel bad, the feeling bad at having felt good—and then there was on top of it the bigger lie about the bottom of the ninth and giving it all you had on every pitch like it was the last pitch, because even though Harry had told his mother he'd been giving it all he had to get the one last man, he had not. Oh, he could throw a lot harder, Harry said to Tom, said he guessed if he wanted to, said he could probably break his mother's wrist if he really let loose and winged one in there the way he knew he could if he only had a catcher who would hang in there and catch it.

Harry watched Tom lean back on the lawn chair he was sitting on and tip the chip bag to get out the last of the crumbs, Tom saying, "If, if, and if" into the bottomed-out hollow of the rattling bag.

Harry licked the chip salt from off his fingers. He rinsed his mouth out with mimosa and pinched a dip of snuff from the chew can in his pocket. He loaded up his lower lip, spitting and saying that he was just saying he could throw a lot harder is all. Harry picked up his father's mitt his mother was using and listened to Tom not believing Harry could throw any harder, Tom asking Harry why would he anyway want to throw the ball that hard at his mother anyhow? did Harry forget already those welts of broken vessels in her hand? the baseball lacing just this day imprinted into her wrist? not to say word one about the places on her she often after the right number of mimosas pulled down her pants and up her shirt to show to Harry and Tom, who had to turn their heads to keep from seeing either the prunes-in-cottage-cheese color of the bruises in her flesh, or the newspaper yellow of her four-hook brassiere, and the sag of slickish underwear worn too big and sure to shake a scare into the illusions of any growing boy who looked too long. "Look at this!" she'd say. "And this!" she'd say. "Did you ever believe a body could bruise so bad? I'm a banana," Harry's mother would say, "a regular mush of tropical fruit. Make up your mother another mimosa, Harry," she'd say, "and how about we play some cards now? How about a few quick games of blackjack?" But Harry rarely let them play cards but said instead that he was in training, a single-minded baseball pitcher bent on more than backyard glory. "This is the majors!" he'd say. "This is the All Stars, the World Series," he'd say, "this is the bottom of the ninth, 1963!" Harry would say and say, getting them all to saying it themselves, maybe even to believing it themselves, believing in the all-or-nothing nature of the thing they did so strongly that Tom now said it seemed more and more certainly to him that Harry never held back so much as a breath in the pitches that he threw, but that he used his legs and back and skinny whip of arm to grind his teeth and let it fly. And if that wasn't true, Tom said, and if Harry really wanted to throw the way he said he knew he could, then why didn't Harry let Tom catch? why didn't Harry let Tom take the place behind the plate, hold up for Harry the big target of Harry's father's major-league mitt?

Harry slipped the chew can back into his back pocket on the circle-worn side. He pincered open and shut the stiff-leathered crawdad claw of his father's mitt. Harry spit out a sluicing arc of tobacco juice any pine-riding minor leaguer would envy, saying, "Why? Because she can't pitch and she can't hit either is why! If she wants to play the game, she's got to play by the rules is why! And besides all that, she likes it!" Harry said, Harry saying to Tom, "Watch this!" and hollering, wise-guy style, shouting, "How you doing?" through the window screen to his mother he knew would now be microwave-thawing out the frozen T-bones in the kitchen. "I said, how's your elbow!" Harry shouted. "I mean, hey, your wrist! I mean, suck it up, sport! Bottom of the ninth!" Harry shouted, taking off his father's mitt and pulling up out of the ice chest another bottle of champagne, thumbing the cork to the critical point, then shooting the cork thooping over the side neighbor's slump-stone wall.

"Bottom of the ninth!" said Harry's mother through the kitchen screen. "T-bones coming up," she said. "What'll it be tonight, men?" said Harry's mother, coming out with a platter in each hand, elbowing open the sliding glass door, asking Harry to make his mother up another mimosa.

Harry made up his mother a mostly champagne mimosa, champagne mostly because he thought he could see his mother thinking blackjack for the night, or poker, or pinochle, or crazy eights, or go fish—any easy gamble to get herself out of having to catch the second game—any old card game Harry knew he and Tom could in short order clean Harry's mother out in if she got again to where she could not even see the deck that Harry was dealing from.

Harry's mother set the T-bones down to sizzle on the grill. Harry gave Tom the eye to let him know what was what, what it was being having to get Harry's mother past the place of the high-fiving champ and into the shoes of the champagne-headed celebrant without stopping off in the middle place, where she would get herself all long-faced and weepy-seeming, sad, a drag, no more sport, but an ordinary woman wanting always to talk about the problems in her past that Harry figured it was high time she passed out of. No more time for ordinary! If he and Tom had told her about how to use the webbed part of the mitt a hundred billion times, then they had warned her off her ass-dragging around the house about a hundred zillion times more than that! Nobody loves a loser. Nobody wants to hear it. And especially not Harry and Tom, who had already heard it just as many jillion times as they had told her not to tell it. Speed was the game! No time for talk! Put up or shut up! Play ball! Don't forget, bottom of the ninth, 1963!

Harry lifted up his plastic cup.

"Drink up!" Harry said. "Here's to us all!"

Just think of it—Mimosas! T-bones! Cole slaw and the ridged-type dippers! A fresh can of chew and a brand-new light for the night game of their first doubleheader! So close, so close!

It was too good to look at and too good not to see, the only hard part in any of it being hoping your mother did not drink too much, but hoping still she didn't drink too little. It was rounding third base and getting the no-slide signal, taking the final coasting turn for home to make a standup score. It was Harry hearing already his mother skip over her ass-dragging past, Harry's mother moving herself straight into the here-and-now and onto Harry, going at him again about the staining dangers of tobacco, pulling down her lower lip to show to Harry her teeth and gums, Harry's mother saying to Harry how the tobacco would discolor everything, rot, even. "You want your teeth to fall out?" she wanted to know. "Look at my wrist," said Harry's mother. "Can you see this? You want your gums to be the color of my wrist? Or of my leg?" said Harry's mother. "Hey, did I show you my leg?" she said.

"No," said Harry. "You didn't show me your leg. You'd better just keep that leg to yourself," Harry said. "And if you really want me to see your wrist," he said, "then I'll have to turn the light on. Otherwise," said Harry, "what you ought to do is soak that wrist until after we all eat."

But they did not the all of them eat. Tom ate. Harry ate. But Harry's mother did not eat, Harry's mother being taken lately to saying she was watching her figure by means of a liquid diet she said it was helping her to lose to be on. So she drank. It was fine so far as the cards went on the nights when she drank, but somewhere in the middle of her fourth, fifth, or sixth mimosa it came to Harry's head the idea his mother might not keep herself in any kind of shape to take her place behind the plate. It came to Harry's head the idea that maybe he and Tom ought not to have eaten the meaty halves of her T-bone the way that she had told them to do, leaving her to gnaw the skimpy part where she assured them the meat was always sweeter next to. "Really," she said, "this is all I need. You boys eat. Eat," she said. "There's plenty," she said. "Plenty more where this came from."

Harry put his mitt on. He ate his ice cream from his mitt, holding the bowl deep in the pocket. He watched Tom eating his ice cream the same way, and watched his mother keeping on her liquid diet, cutting out now the orange-juice part without this time even blaming it on what she called the acidic condition of her stomach. Harry heard Tom start in to scraping his spoon against his bowl, a sound sadder to Harry than the emptiest bag of the best ridged dippers. Harry saw his mother unwinding the wires from around the top of another champagne bottle. Harry and Tom looked first one at the other and then back at Harry's mother, who was aiming the bottle off in the direction of the side neighbor's slump-stone wall, thumbing the cork and shooting it off over to where she had always told Harry and Tom to please stop shooting them, the cork disappearing out into the darkness Harry could no longer see through. His mother filled herself up. Harry picked up the baseball and began to snap the ball into his mitt, where the finished-up ice-cream bowl wasn't anymore.

What they had going here was not a full count. This was not two outs, bottom of the ninth, bases loaded. There was no last pitch here. There was no last man. This was not the bottom of the ninth, 1963. What they had going here was a momentum stopper, a rally killer, what was occurring to Harry as the sudden buggish itching so much silence in his mother gave him.

Harry said, "Don't you want to play some cards?"

"No," said Harry's mother. "No, I think I better rest."

"That's right," said Tom. "You better rest."

"Rest?" Harry said. "That's it? Rest?"

"Rest," said Harry's mother. "For the next game," she said.

"All right," Harry said. "Good, then, you just rest. Ice your wrist, why don't you? I think I'll turn on the light."

"Can you wait?" Harry's mother said. "Let me finish resting? Can you wait a little while? Give me ten more minutes?"

Harry bumped his thumb along the baseball's raised-up stitching. He smacked the ball against the cement porch. He caught the ball off the rebound, and said he guessed he didn't see right off why not he couldn't wait another ten more minutes. Harry watched his mother put her champagne cup into the big-league pocket of his father's mitt to have another mimosa out of from. Tom stuck out his mitt, too, and wondered whether might he have another along with Harry's mother so long as all they were doing was resting.

It was the kind of a thing you had to see it to believe it, Harry's mother needing not to play a game of cards to keep from playing ball, needing not to fill the quiet times of the night with all the used-up words she'd thrown out all of those hundred billion times before. Harry leaned back on his lawn chair to look up at the blank sky blackening above him. He tapped his mitt against his leg, trying to figure back to how many heartbeats ago it was when waiting was easy.

Another ten more minutes!

How many seconds in another ten more minutes? Ten times sixty seconds is how many! Six hundred seconds! You just tap your mitt against your leg another six hundred more times, Harry, and we'll be ready! You just let us rest until you can count the first six hundred stars to come out tonight and we'll play ball. Give us another six hundred swallows and we'll be primed for the night game of this here backyard doubleheader.

Harry reloaded up his lower lip. He arced a perfect spitter out onto the lawn and muscled up his tongue for the locker-room lashing he could see his team was in sore need of. Then he stood up from out of the lawn chair and started in to pacing the cement porch, socking now his fist, now the baseball into his mitt, beginning by saying to his mother and Tom that never to Harry's knowing had there ever been a single Hall of Famer made famous on the strength of waiting and resting. Never had Harry heard of a time where the winner said he owed his crown to a blood-rare slab of T-bone meat and another ten more minutes to digest it in peace. Imagine it! Imagine, Harry said, the one last man waiting while you rested in the dark, slamming down the champagne, digesting the food to fuel the next last pitch you expected to strike him out again with, asking the one last man to please wait, to sit still awhile, to let you rest a bit before you caught him flat-footed with the final strike. "Fat chance!" he said. "This isn't little league! This isn't the minors! This is the big leagues, the majors!" Harry said, "the bottom of the ninth, 1963!" he said.

So what did Tom say?

"See what your mother says," said Tom.

And what did Harry's mother say?

"It's hard, Harry," said Harry's mother. "I'm tired. It's hard, honey," she said, "playing two games."

So who ever said it would be easy?

Listen, what did you have to do with a mother like this!

What you had to do for openers was you had to leave your best friend and only mother sitting soft-headed from too much champagne drunk in the dark to start yourself to throwing against your side neighbor's slump-stone wall. You had to start off like to finish, throwing from the get-go the kind of wall chippers that when the other guy heard cracking off the slump stone he got too scared to take the bat in hand to face you. What you had to do was to keep on playing hard until the other guy dropped, then keep on playing harder. You had to convince yourself. You had to knock a wall down. You needed to be able each time to reach back and throw the high, hard one and hit the mark on the slump-stone wall that would send the ball right back to where you wanted it to go so as to pick it up and do it

45

again. You had to work the hitch out from your windup, perfect the rhythm of your stride. You did it with your eyes closed. You did it in the dark. You had to learn to live inside yourself in a world where there was no time to wake up what might have died inside you. You had already to be in a sweat. You needed to show to Tom and to your mother the only reason to fill up the way they did was to burn it all off in the playing of the next game, and then the next, until the last game had been played out and was in the record books for good and all.

But what Harry missed seeing in six hundred seconds of slump-stone wall bashing, and what he saw when Tom called him over was not Tom and his mother with mitts on and making ready to take the field for the second game, but Harry's mother and Tom still laid up in the locker room, three-quarters crocked on the lawn chair benches, sunk deeper than ever into a postchampagne disarray, his mother not saying anything or even making a twitch of a move to raise her head up from where it was buried down deep between her knees.

"I think she's sick," said Tom.

"Sick?" said Harry.

"Said she's feeling sort of puny."

"Puny?"

"Puny," Tom said, Tom standing what Harry guessed Tom must have thought to be a good safe distance from Harry's mother to wait and watch and see what next.

"The light," said Harry. "What we need here is a little light on the subject."

Harry saw his mother lift her head to squint against the light and see him standing at the switch, and it didn't look good, the little bit of her what Harry saw before his mother's head dropped back down between her knees. Harry circled around his mother to approach her from behind, and with his pitching hand he gathered together a fistful of her hair, while with his glove hand he lifted her up by her listless shoulder. Harry's mother's jaw fell down when her head came up, and the dim-wittedest bat boy could have seen that the problem was not entirely too much champagne but had probably more exactly to do with the specks of chewing tobacco he saw stuck all on her teeth.

"You gave her a chew?" Harry said.

"She said she wanted one," said Tom. "She said she wanted to spit like we did."

Harry turned his mother's head toward himself. It seemed to him that her skin was getting to be a sort of a cadaverous color by the light of the light that Harry began to see would not this night be used for the second game of the doubleheader they had planned to play, Harry's mother saying now that yes, she didn't guess she felt so good. Could Harry help her to the toilet? Could he help his mother to her feet?

Harry helped his mother, noticing, as he hoisted her up, his mother's wrist, the only living color on her body that he could see, her wrist still—how many hours now?—showing the cross-hatched stitching red in the center of a patch of purple swollen almost to the size of the baseball Harry had thrown to make it that way.

"I think it's broken, dear," Harry's mother said.

"I don't think so," Harry said.

"Might be," Tom said.

"Maybe a chip," Harry said. "But not a break."

47

"It's broken, dear," Harry's mother said. She said, "Hurry."

They made it to the toilet, Harry and his mother, with Tom tagging along to make sure, Tom saying it sounded to him like there was some serious porcelain prayer going on inside there, some major-league heaving for sure. Lucky for her, Tom was saying, she hadn't eaten the way he and Harry had. "Could you imagine it," Tom wanted to know, "a T-bone coming up? Or how about those chips?" Tom said. "Double lucky for her she didn't eat any of those ridged dippers," he said. But even still with the luck and all, Tom supposed it was a rookie move, Harry's mother getting sick like that from off of only the half-pinch of tobacco that he had given to her.

"Yours was the rookie move," Harry said, Harry saying to Tom that Tom had done exactly what Harry's mother had wanted him to do. "She's a veteran," Harry said. "She got you soft. She got you to sitting in the dark with women. Did she tell you one game was enough?" Harry said. "Did she tell you you couldn't do it all? That you had to make a choice? Listen up," Harry said to Tom. "Champions never choose."

Harry put his ear against the door to hear his mother finishing up losing the rest of what she didn't have to lose.

"Are you all right?" Harry asked his mother. "Are you drowning in there?"

"No," said Harry's mother. "No, I'm not drowning. I'm getting my second wind. I'm getting ready for this second game. I'm brushing my teeth. Are you ready?" she said. "How's your arm?" she said.

Her second wind!

Could you beat it? Could you beat the Babe, the Mick, Maris, or Mays? She was coming out from the toilet to play the second game! And this, try beating this—try topping the picture of Harry's mother, coming out of the bathroom like to take the field after only the seventh-inning stretch, taking, too, a fast hold of Harry's ear to drag him along and tell him that if he wanted to see a champion to come on out and try her. Top Harry hung up by his ear, top him tiptoed and never for an instant trying to pull out from his mother's grip, Harry remembering in her pinch of callused finger pads how strong this woman who filled out a four-hook brassiere could really be.

Who here was the champ? Who here didn't have what it took to take the bat in hand? Just ask Tom, who was telling Harry he'd just as soon sit it out on the lawn chair bench for this one, Harry's mother telling Harry not even should he think about sitting it out, telling him to shut up his mouth and pick up his mitt to start this night game she was sick of hearing how much he had been saying he wanted to play so bad. "Come on!" she said. "Bottom of the ninth!" Harry's mother said. "Let's play ball, Drake!"

Here it was! Here they were! The classic matchup! Here was Harry on the mound, there his mother behind the plate, the both of them alone and under the light at last!

Harry kicked his cleat against the rubber. He squeezed the ball inside his mitt. He passed his arm across his forehead and stared down at his mother squatted out there on her haunches. Harry could taste it in his arm, the blood-rare flavor of red meat, as he studied the target his mother held up for him to throw at, Harry set already to shake off the signals he expected his mother to give him. No chance of this night throwing anything like a change-of-pace—no, he would stick with the heat, throwing fastballs to show to Tom, to show to her, what smoke could look like, what real fire could sound like when it left Harry's hand and blazed a straight line through the night to split the plate, a leathered splat in his father's big-league mitt, the sound of the champion nailing down the one last man.

But never did Harry see his mother signal for a single change-of-pace, but he heard her holler instead for him to throw still harder, Harry beginning to turn loose now the kind of slump-stone wall chippers he could not believe he was really throwing, could not believe his mother would really have the stuff to catch.

His mother did not bail out. She did not blink. Nor did she quit with her chatter—but called out to Harry that he would never get the one last man if what he had thrown so far was the best he had. "Bush league!" she shouted. "Rag arm!" she screamed. She didn't even need a mitt, she said, to catch his limp-wristed pitches. "It's gone!" she said. "Over the wall, out of the park!" she yelled—and she did it, in a single easy motion Harry saw her do it, saw his mother throw his father's mitt up and over onto the dark side of the slump-stone wall Harry had all summer tried to throw through.

Harry took his time. He worked the ball in his hand, trying to find the right killer grip for the next last pitch he found he could not throw, Harry feeling in each of the raised-up stitches the first mark to be struck in his big-league record under the column for losses. He saw his mother waving and clapping her bare-skinned hands, saw his mother rock down now from her haunches to her knees,

Harry's mother asking him what was wrong, why didn't he throw, what was the matter, couldn't he see, couldn't he see her?

"Can't you see?" she said. "Hey, Drake! Can't you see me?" his mother said. "Come on, baby, burn it in here! Show us what you've got! Let's get this lousy man! Come on, can you see me, champ? Come on," she said. "You know you can see me. I'm here, baby—here is your mother, sonny boy!"

Reno, Reno, Reno, Reno

ALL THIS that had happened happened, Harry recalled, back in the almost forgotten time of the town when the roads were dirt and the people were broke and hoping.

It's what made the dog historical.

"Tragicomic," Harry would say, and rap the top of the old dog's head with his balled-up knuckles, citing the animal's blinking, half-blind, cataract eyes as artifactual truth. "Tragicomic," Harry would repeat, this being his own newliest way of naming the tale. Harry would close his eyes, wag his head from side to side. "Somebody," he would say, "ought to make up a docudrama about that damn tragicomedy," meaning not about the dog whose head Harry rapped, but about what all it was had happened with his mother's long since, tragicomically, dead dog, Spivey, mother of the dog at the foot of Harry's chair, Spivey, the little bit of a bitch who had whelped herself on into history; and, too, about the one man who had come around their house so much in that time, the man who was—among all the other broke and hoping people who had come around their house—the most full of hope, was, in fact, to hear Harry's mother tell it, punch-drunk on hope, but who, after Harry's father's straight-faced way of seeing things, was just plain old ordinarily and everyday drunk —Mr. Oates.

They would see Mr. Oates, Harry, and his forever best friend Tom, from where they were busy on some summer day, practicing up on their drawing of naked women in the just-raked dirt of the unlawned yard. It was an easy thing, spotting out Mr. Oates from all the others, there being no vehicle in that time, not even Harry's father's, could raise the same dust as that one-ton flatbed Ford. From clear down at the corner they all called back then Jack's Ditch in honor after the man who rolled his pickup there, Harry and Tom would see Mr. Oates and get up off of their knees, squinting to see the dust come closer.

"Here now!" Harry's mother would shout from the house. "You two get out of that yard. You know we just seeded that dirt!"

And Harry and Tom would drop their sticks and sprint on down the crushed-gravel drive with Spivey in tow, the dog's four dachshund—they all said dashhound—four dashhound legs a churning blur under her sleek weenie body.

"Spivey!" Harry's mother would scream. "Spivey! You, Harry! You, Tom! Catch that dog if it's that man coming!"

But they never did try to catch Spivey, Harry and Tom, them knowing firstly each of the other that had they been even able to catch her, they were just as likely to tear out her brown-furred throat as to fetch her back up to the house to Harry's mother. What else and secondly it was that Harry and Tom knew—and what accounted for Spivey's crooked-looking head, the crown somehow not lining up with the jaw underneath—was that Spivey was not a dog to go for a rolling truck. It was the parked trucks Spivey had loved, and it had been Harry's father's unlucky luck to back over Spivey asleep in the shade under the big rear tire, mashing Spivey's dashhound head into the crushed-gravel drive.

"Spivey was a survivor," Harry would say of Spivey's tire-mashed head. With the sole of his shoe Harry would stroke the back of his own dog, son of Spivey, sleeping now maybe on the barroom floor. "For a dashhound," Harry would say, "Spivey was a real clinger-onner."

It was on account of her being mad in love with Mr. Oates's truck, Harry figured, mad in love with what rode up on the flatbed part of his one-ton Ford, that kept Spivey in a surviving frame of mind.

"Never seen a she-dog did it that way," Mr. Oates had yelled over the idle of his engine.

Harry and Tom, chests heaving still from the sprint down the drive, would grin, watching Spivey cock her leg to mark as hers each one of Mr. Oates's six tires—four in the back, two up front.

"Which one of you two taught her that trick?" said Mr. Oates.

"He did," Harry said.

"He did," Tom said.

"That's what I figured," Mr. Oates said.

Mr. Oates would shut down his engine then, have himself another swallow from the bottle, pulling his lips up over his teeth and gums the way Harry and Tom had liked to see. Mr. Oates would jack the mirror over, slicken with spit his hair straight back on his head. Harry and Tom saw it as a habit of Mr. Oates's, his getting himself all spruced up that way, asking after Harry's father, asking after Harry's mother, then wiping his scratched plastic sunglasses on his T-shirted shoulder. Harry and Tom would wait, watch Mr. Oates climb out and down from his truck, both of them wondering what it was this time that Mr. Oates might have in his big closed-up hands, both of them keeping an eye on Mr. Oates's black-haired knuckles, waiting to feel the thick fleshed press of the inside part of his fisted hand that was someway softer, finer than any of the other men's hands the two had ever before been made to shake with.

"Stick out your mitts, men," Mr. Oates would say, and Harry and Tom would hold out their hands to shake with Mr. Oates, sometimes getting in change for their shakes a piece of gum in their palms, sometimes a silver dollar, sometimes a rock or else a lump of hot tar.

If it was the gum or the dollar, Harry and Tom would thank Mr. Oates and run back to doing whatever it was they had been at; if the rock or the tar, they would chuck one or the other or both at once at Spivey, who barked and yapped and would never shut up, leaping and panting in the way that she had, horsing after what most in the town at that time had called the ugliest dog around—a mongrel, a scamp, a two-bit trashcan tipper, Mr. Oates's dog, who Mr. Oates for his own unique reasons called just that, called Dog, said, "I believe in calling a dog Dog," said, "Damn, Dog, you get off his leg," said, "Damn, Dog, pull your nose from her crotch," said, "Lord, Dog, you smell bad"—Dog, who rode on top of whichever it was Mr. Oates would be hauling, be it railroad ties, cinder blocks, tire rims, or bags of fertilizer all stacked up tall on the flatbed planks—the raw materials for his most current project, his latest great hope.

"What do you got, Mr. Oates?" Harry had asked. "What do you got?"

"Got pipe," said Mr. Oates.

"Pipe!" said Tom.

"Pipe?" said Harry.

"Secret," said Mr. Oates.

"Shit, secret!" said Harry and Tom both, and followed Mr. Oates up to the house and Harry's mother, crossing across the rake-lined dirt of the newly seeded yard.

Mr. Oates tucked in his T-shirt while walking, jerked his thumb back over his shoulder toward his truck and dog and Spivey still barking and said, "What is it do you two suppose about her makes that dog of mine so bashful?"

It was the question, Harry remembered, Mr. Oates had asked most, and the question Harry and Tom always shouted to answer, answering, "She loves the big Dog! She loves the big Dog!"

And it was true, seeing the way that Spivey had torn the ears and gone for the throats on her own size and smaller. Three times previous Harry's mother had tried to breed Spivey toward a right and proper whelping, Harry's mother having in mind AKC-papered puppies, future blue ribbons, plain green cash. It was the part of Harry's mother—her big ideas with Spivey's future breeding—that Harry's father would later say had made her such a sucker for Mr. Oates's own brand of altruistic money making. It was the part of Harry's mother—her big ideas, her constant wanting after something fine—that Harry's father would later say had made her soft, whipped and beaten before the game began.

But all of that was neither here nor there, Harry would say, because Spivey was not buying any part of any one of those thin-nosed, long-bodied, blue-blooded dashhound suitors, but had been busy saving herself up for something bigger, something rougher, wilder, a real dog's dog, that being, as it happened, Mr. Oates's dog, Dog, who, as history had recorded on the first time of his and Spivey's meeting, beat his tail-tucked ass fast back up to the top of the stacked wooden pallets he had on that long-gone day rode in on.

"She wants the big dog!" Harry and Tom had shouted then, "She wants the big Dog!" they shouted now while following Mr. Oates on up the unlawned yard, pausing only for Mr. Oates to compliment Tom's artistic artistry on the picture of the naked lady drawn into the dirt, recommending only hair, "There's hair down there," he said, "unless of course you boys find yourselves a little something eastern," Mr. Oates had said, causing Harry and Tom to wonder aloud to each other why it might be that the ones from Utah, say, or Colorado even, would not have the same hair the girls out here in the West had.

"Here now!" Harry's mother screamed again from the house. "You three get out of that yard! You, Mr. Oates, is that dog of yours tied?"

"Yes, ma'am," called Mr. Oates, his thumbs retucking his T-shirt, running under his belt and around the circumference of his sucked-in belly. "Though I don't think that dog of mine has got it in his head to move anywhere near to where that little weenie could lay her paws on him."

"That dashhound's name is Spivey," Harry's mother said. "And anyway look at what you've done to my yard."

Harry, Tom, and Mr. Oates all looked back to the perfect prints of their shoes in the soft seeded dirt.

"Have you got a rake handy?" said Mr. Oates.

"No, no," said Harry's mother. "Don't you worry," she said, "I'll get to it soon as I've finished pulling the sage out back."

Mr. Oates said, "You ought to get you some sod."

"Sod," said Harry's mother. "Who can afford sod?"

"The Kratzers down the road for one," said Mr. Oates.

"The Kratzers?" Harry's mother said. "The Kratzers?"

"Just this morning," said Mr. Oates. "I saw the Mexicans rolling it out."

"Oh, fine," said Harry's mother. "Must be nice to have that kind of money. I don't suppose it hurts them any to know that they still owe us for that extra bedroom we built on for them. I don't suppose it hurts them to see that we and every other on this block have got to fight with seed. I don't suppose they care about birds or wind or dogs or kids? Fine," Harry's mother said, "just fine. Must be nice."

Harry watched Mr. Oates pass his hand over his spit-slicked hair.

"Well," said Mr. Oates.

"Spivey's named out of spite," Harry said then.

"Quiet," Harry's mother said.

"That's what my dad said," said Harry. "It used to be my mom's name before she took ours," Harry said.

Harry's mother grabbed Harry's shoulder, pulled him tight to her side.

"So," she said, "what is it this time, Mr. Oates? I see you've got pipe."

Mr. Oates had pipe, Harry remembered. With anyone else who had come by their house in that time, Harry would have guessed from the pipe probably plain toilet plumbing or maybe backyard irrigation. *Simple, economic, solid,* and *practical* were the words back then the most of them that came to Harry's father in asking for help had used. But never once to Harry's knowing had those words or any of their kind ever come from the mouth of Mr. Oates. Mr. Oates, Harry recalled, had himself a knack for making the clear cloudy, mountains out of molehills, what he himself called making good things better, real life into dreams.

"What," Harry would ask, this by way of example while telling the tale to whoever it was he had roped into hearing, this time, say, sitting with his old dog on the soggy redwood benches, the two of them there with hung tongues, sweating off a two-day hangover in the YMCA sauna bath, "what," Harry would ask, "would you think of AstroTurf and concrete, say?"

Miniature golf would for that question be the right guess. Miniature golf it had been that first caught Harry's mother's heart, and in turn Harry's father's ear, all of them soon after—Harry, his mother, his father, Tom, and Mr. Oates—spending their afterwork and weekend time in building the front nine of what Mr. Oates had claimed would be the Augusta, the Firestone, the Pebble Beach of miniature golf courses—what Mr. Oates had said ought, if anything at all, to be called Spiveyland—an attraction sure to add pride and prestige to the growth of the town, as well as grab the wallets of every other four-doored, station-wagoned, north-south-bound passerby on 395. And it might have done just what Mr. Oates had hoped it could have done—if only not for the bog, or not exactly the bog itself, which had looked harmless enough in winter and on into the early part of spring, but the mosquitoes that had hatched out from the bog and drove the players away, needle-nosed and feasting in the pre-bluelight-bug-zapping time of the town when the short-sleeved, bare-legged limbs of the miniature golfers were for the mosquitoes a sun-baked smorgasbord.

Harry, Tom, Harry's mother, and Mr. Oates had all worked the course and watched the way it had slipped away. They had seen at first families too many to count, and then too few to matter, leaning over putters in the thick mosquito haze, slapping themselves stupid, opting not to buy the mosquito stuff Mr. Oates had had the bright idea to supply, but to instead keep on down the road, heading for the bowling alleys, or else the air-conditioned, completely bug-free movies. Even the free-game winners, Harry remembered—the ones who knocked the orange balls between the opening and closing jaws of the giant dashhound head—kept on and kept on not coming back, until the cash ran out, and the banks complained, and Spiveyland shut down for good.

But Spiveyland, Harry would say, was only the tip of what was worse than an iceberg.

There had been, Harry would say, horseshoe pits and batting cages, a dance hall and a roller rink. There had

been a roping arena, and a combination mineral-spa-slash-
go-cart-track. There had been, of course, a merry-go-
round. There had been even more, Harry remembered,
though he did not remember exactly what all in particular,
and there had been better-than-mosquito reasons for why
each of these projects had failed the same way Spiveyland
had failed, the particular reasons here, too, Harry choosing
to disremember—though when pushed supposed it had
most likely to do with Mr. Oates's not passing out names
to all of what he built, Mr. Oates's notion here being in
keeping with what caused him to call Dog Dog—the idea
that a name brought no luck, that a thing was never quite
all it might be once it had a title fixed to it.

Mr. Oates would say, "I'd rather if I had to just hang
up a picture of what the place is."

What Harry did remember was Mr. Oates—Mr. Oates's
hope.

Harry remembered Mr. Oates always arriving fresh off
the heels of his latest defeat—sometimes even before
defeat—raising dust around Jack's Ditch and on up the
dirt road to their house, his flatbed Ford stacked up high,
Dog on top, Mr. Oates's chin held up as he came to a stop,
his breath sweet from the bottle, saying, "Boys, the sure-
firedest sign of a grown-up town is play. Mark my words,
you two," Mr. Oates would say, "play is the greatest thing
a human being can do. We can sell it."

It was hard going, even for Mr. Oates, convincing Harry's father on that count about play, it being Harry's father's own personal view that work was what it was that
made a person great. In fact, Harry would say, most likely
none of it that had happened would have happened had it

not been for the prospect of some profit, the first heartfelt words from Harry's mother, and the everyman's natural disinclination to go ahead and cut his losses and walk away from a sinking ship. But then, too, Harry would say, it could have been the simpler fact of plain old Mr. Oates— the man, the promise in his handshake, the aspect in his eye, the unflagging belief that he, Mr. Oates, had seen what the rest of the town ought on their better days to have wanted to see.

So it was pipe, Harry would say, that Mr. Oates had arrived with as the latest way of saving the day, raising the ship, floating the boat.

"Tell us, Mr. Oates!" Harry had cried. "Tell us what you're going to do with the pipe!"

But Mr. Oates did not say what was what with the pipe, but said instead what he always said, which was, "What makes the game is not knowing the end," a thing neither Harry nor Tom ever understood except through Harry's mother, who would say by way of translation, "Too many chiefs and not enough Indians."

"Oh, we were Indians, all right," Harry would say. Harry would smile, remembering himself and Tom, and reach out his hand to unsnag his old dog's upper lip from his bottom broken tooth. "Me and Tom," Harry would say, "we were regular Comanches."

It was one-half the two of them being Indians, Harry recalled, one-half Spivey being Spivey that had landed them then with the chore of the yard.

"Look!" Harry's mother had said. "My God, Mr. Oates, look how that flea-bitten hound of yours has upset my Spivey!"

They all looked, and it was plain to see that Spivey had
it bad for Dog. There could be no doubting the flying wake
of seed she dug, the crazy eights and circles she was making
through the just-raked dirt, and the way her hind legs
nearly overreached the front, almost clearing the length of
her dashhound body, her teeth, too, shown grinning
slightly off of center from under her pumping head, gaining
momentum to take another wild and reckless leap, only to
slam herself just above the hubcap—inches, feet, miles
away from the one, now howling, Dog that she loved.

"My God!" Harry's mother said. "Just look at what that
dog of yours is making her do to my yard! Is that beast of
yours deficient? How on earth did he get so ugly?"

"It's generic, ma'am," said Mr. Oates.

"Generic!" said Harry's mother. "You mean *genetic!*"

"Well, ma'am," said Mr. Oates, "I guess I know what
I mean."

"Well, you meant genetic," said Harry's mother.

"I only said what I meant," said Mr. Oates.

"You meant *generic?*" said Harry's mother.

"If you say so," said Mr. Oates.

"Oh, my God," said Harry's mother. "You think it's
funny, Harry? Tom? You'll think funny," she said. "Mr.
Oates," Harry's mother said, "have you got chicken wire
on your truck?"

"Yes, ma'am," said Mr. Oates.

"Rebar?"

"Yes, ma'am."

"A single jack?"

"Yes, ma'am."

"Then that settles it," said Harry's mother. "If you two

boys have got nothing better to do than to hang around here causing trouble the whole day long, then you can set yourselves to building me a fence. Mr. Oates," she said, "you get these boys started, and then come on up and tell me what you've got in mind with that pipe."

Mr. Oates, Harry recalled, had set him and Tom up that day with a rebar cutter and a posthole digger, a tape measure and tin snips, dikes, wire, and gloves. Mr. Oates gave them later a seed spreader with a shoulder bag and a turn crank. On another day Mr. Oates had showed up with an invention of his very own making—a scaled-down version of his one-ton Ford, a sprinkler on wheels, a self-propelled water truck that watered the dirt along its track of hose in the time of the town when the people—even the Kratzers down the road—were still ape-faced over Whirlibirds and Rainbows. Keeping the fence, raking, reseeding, and watering—it all got to be from that point on Harry's and Tom's job to turn the dirt into grass, to catch the grass up to the Kratzers's store-bought sod. Lucky for himself and Tom, Harry would say, to have had Mr. Oates to help get them started, Mr. Oates teaching them in each way the best way, the easy way.

"I'll tell you what, boys," Mr. Oates would say, "they may laugh at you, they might talk behind your back—but I'll swear it to you again—the easy way is the best way. Never force a thing to where it doesn't want to go. Make your work play," Mr. Oates would say, "and you'll live the life of Reilly, you'll be in like Flynn."

Mr. Oates would shake their hands, slipping Harry and Tom sometimes the good, sometimes the bad, taking one last swig, slicking his hair and tucking in his T-shirt, then squinting over the tops of his scratched plastic sunglasses, far on down the old dirt road and clear to Jack's Ditch, asking the two of them, Harry and Tom, to please give a holler when they saw Harry's father, before heading up the crushed-gravel drive on his way to the house to see Harry's mother to talk about pipe.

Harry and Tom would be left alone then with their goods to keep and their bads to chuck, skipping the stones and the lumps of hot tar off the misshapen head of Spivey, who had since become an easy shot, sleeping the way that she did now under the big back tires of Mr. Oates's truck, Mr. Oates having shown Harry and Tom how a dog that foamed at the mouth like Spivey foamed had to have had itself a hell of a thirst to quench, Mr. Oates then showing the two of them the way just a little splash from the liquor bottle mixed in with her water would do the trick and knock her out, quieting Spivey's love-crazed dashhound yap.

Not that Spivey had always lived in the female grip.

"No, sir," Harry would say, continuing his tale after maybe making apologies for the nose-burning bad gas his old dog had just passed—"It's the new food," Harry would explain to the person most current who listened, "I got a good buy on a fifty-pound bag of bad Kibble bits"—and he would fan the air with his hand, saying, "No, sir—not a bit of the sissy. Spivey ran with the boys."

All through the mornings and into the early part of the afternoons before Mr. Oates and Dog showed up, Spivey had chased with Harry and Tom up and down the gullies and fields that were in that time the backyard playground of the place where they had all grown up. They would rise

and shine with the sun, Tom meeting Harry and Spivey at
Harry's house to spread the seed and set the water truck
on its track of hose, turning it to low, to slow, to give them
the time they would need to slip away for the day, raising
the first plumes of dust up the unpaved road, ditching their
bikes at the top of the hill, going it fast on foot and on
paw down the slope where the onions grew wild, then back
up the other side of the gully, through the tall, dew-covered
sage that wetted their jeans and smelled nearly like rain,
clear up and higher to the cottonwood tree with the swing
and the house, mounting the rungs nailed into the trunk,
up and up to the plywood top—above the ditch and the
gully, the sage and the onions, above their houses, the town
in the valley—clear up from where they could still see the
miles across to the eastern ranges where the sun had
climbed in a sky Harry would grow up and call the truest
blue he ever saw.

They would watch, Harry remembered, from way up
there, counting the dust-raising comings and goings of
pickups and cars making the corner at Jack's Ditch—how
many stopping off at Harry's house, how many at Tom's.
From way up there, they could see the places where the
tractors and trucks were just starting up—smoke and more
dust—new roads being graded, new houses being built.
From way up there each would try to guess at which site
his own father worked—listening, even, to the big engine
sounds and the whine and whack of hammers and saws;
and then they would give up, looking again to the ranges
in the east, saying how small, really, how tiny, those tractors and trucks, and wondering whether that was Utah
they were seeing in the east, or Colorado, and speculating,

from way up where they were, on those hairless girls described by Mr. Oates.

It was speculating, Harry remembered, that he and Tom had been hard at on the time Spivey had decided to jump from way up there.

Before Harry, before Tom—and without the swing— Spivey was the first among them to plumb the air, leaving the tree without looking back, her black ears spread wing- like from her tire-mashed head, her seal-slick body striking the swift ditch and sounding off with a dashhound smack. It was something to see, Harry would say, and it had made up for the first ill will he and Tom had felt regarding Spivey's tag-along status, it being Harry's mother's notion that Spivey's toenails might be run off in the hills with the two, Spivey simply refusing to sit still for her toenails to be clipped, which in turn was to Harry's mind further proof—along with every little-dog sweater she ever had shredded, every perfumed bath she had ever rolled off in the dust—of what Harry meant when he said Spivey's way with Dog was not her everyday way, but was a way that required drops from the bottle, knocks on the head from the tar and the rocks.

It was for her own good, Harry would say. Apart from Dog, Harry would say, Spivey was clean and pure, the kind of a dog that if she were a human a person could trust— and, to tell it rightly, Harry had to admit to the times of his and Tom's most secret talks when it seemed to Harry as if Spivey was doing just that, listening, being trusted, cocking and raising her head, pricking her ears and yawn- ing at the high and low points of the half-truths and lies the two had told, Tom bragging on the anatomical cor-

rectness of the naked-lady drawing they had gone ahead
and left unseeded, the clover already outlining in spring-
green leaf the fine curving highlights of breasts and buttocks, Tom saying a guy didn't get that kind of detail except
from having had a hand in the real McCoy; while Harry
answered, Bullshit, what about pictures? drawing was a
kid's game he had already one-upped on Tom, pointing
out then to Tom the famous clump of long blond girl-hair
forever hooked there under the roughed-up plywood where
they were sitting, claiming it was himself, Harry, who had
got that hair to get there, having laid that girl back on her
back and hooking that hair while copping a feel—a real
feel of a real girl breast!

And why not? Why not trust a dog like Spivey?

Spivey, Harry remembered, was at least as much and
often more than what he and Tom had ever been or in
that time had hoped to ever be. Spivey explored and con-
quered. Spivey adventured and killed. Spivey covered five
times the field and gully Harry and Tom had covered and
never once to Harry's knowing lost an ounce of the grit
and sand that gave her pride. Spivey followed the long line
of her dashhound nose and had showed Harry and Tom
much of what they would otherwise never have seen, took
Harry and Tom to the places they would otherwise never
have been. Spivey, Harry remembered, mixed it up, knew
where to look for what was worth finding, and was not
afraid to face it whenever it was found. It was Spivey, Harry
would say, who had showed them the way to the redtail
hawk shocked dead from high up off the power line; and
it had been Spivey's lead that led them to the yipping,
yowling den of already scary-toothed coyote pups. And it

was Spivey, too, who first poked her nose and raced her way down the tunnel to the cavelike place Harry and Tom had dared both each and the other to go on into, having finally had to decide it on a coin flip—Harry losing —then belly-crawling his way down into the dark and soundless place they later came to call the Heart.

"Yes, ma'am," Harry would say, pausing to rest the worn-out bones of his arthritic dog, who trailed along now leash-tied to the supermarket shopping cart, "Yes, ma'am," Harry would say, "maybe it was the size of Spivey's heart that kept her going after Dog."

There was no other explaining it, Harry would say. They would the three of them, Harry remembered—himself and Tom and Spivey—come back down and out of those fields and gullies of their backyard playground, hurrying to greet Mr. Oates and Dog, hurrying to wait to get on with the pipe. There was no other explaining it, Harry would repeat, the way Spivey carried on and what she got in return. It seemed to Harry that the more heroic Spivey's feats, the less Dog noticed. Harry had seen Spivey fight a rockchuck to a standstill, limp bruised and bloodied underneath Dog, who never once raised his head from his dozing in the sun. Harry had seen Spivey parade around and around the one-ton Ford, dragging a rattlesnake clenched in her teeth, Dog only blinking occasionally to wet the eyes that the rising dust had dried. Spivey had another time found herself on the sharp-barbed side of a porcupine, receiving not the sympathetic whinings of Dog, but instead Harry's mother, and the nurse, and the vet, who clipped and yanked the quills, set Spivey back on her feet to go out for more.

But it was not only Spivey who had suffered.

Harry and Tom had come as well to notice the lack of attention paid to them by Mr. Oates. Mr. Oates had left off with the handshakes and surprises, all but forgot Tom's naked lady. There were no new tools to make the way easy, no more inventions to make the work into play. More than once Mr. Oates had showed up not only with none of what Harry and Tom had come to expect, but the kinds of things they might have gotten at the hands of Harry's father. Tools. Dumb tools. Mean tools. Tools that blistered fingers and callused palms. Tools to hide from. The kind of tools that made Harry and Tom hold their stomachs and wish they had never come down from the cottonwood tree and the fields and the gully.

Mr. Oates had showed up with a pick and a shovel.

"I brought trees," Mr. Oates had said to Harry's mother. "Lombardy poplars. They don't look like much now," he had said, "but you'll remember me by them later when the wind blows here."

Mr. Oates had showed up with a hoe and a spade.

"Bulbs," Mr. Oates had said. "Glads and tulips. To help get you past the Kratzers."

Harry's mother, pleased, said, "You're a dear, Mr. Oates. You're a saint."

It was easy to see, Harry would say, that something was not on the up-and-up with Mr. Oates. All through the excavation of whatever it was they were preparing for the pipe, and on into the pouring of the footings, Mr. Oates had taken to changing even the way of his look. Anymore, Harry and Tom hardly ever saw Mr. Oates slick his hair back with spit, nor never did they see him step out of his truck with his T-shirt untucked, and on some days when

Harry and Tom saw Mr. Oates they noticed he was not wearing a T-shirt at all, but a regular shirt with sleeves and buttons, a shirt sometimes ironed to the collar, creased and stiff. They saw, too, Mr. Oates had got for himself a brand-new pair of unscratched sunglasses, and a pocket-sized squirter that made mint and medicine out of the bottle-sweet smell of his breath. In the treehouse, in the fields and gullies, Harry and Tom had talked it over, decided there was a new sort of unfingerable lightness about Mr. Oates's waist, a shavedness about his face, a smell like soap and limes they did not trust.

The whole pace of things, Harry remembered, changed, passed faster, and the sounds of things, too, got quieter. Things were falling into place, Harry remembered, each thing having its own separate place. A place for Spivey, a place for Dog. One place for Harry and Tom, another for Mr. Oates and Harry's mother. Harry's father had his place, and the yard had a fence. But it seemed to Harry when he came to think of it—when he tried to tell all that had happened between the time Mr. Oates had first showed up with pipe, and what came out in the end—that all of the things falling each into its own separate place made for a great running-together, a glossed-over order—an easy thing to forget.

Harry could remember no screaming from his mother. He could remember no new jolts from Mr. Oates. In his mind's eye Harry could not find Spivey doing anything other than sleeping, patiently waiting for her chance at Dog. Even Tom and himself, Harry recalled, had begun to leave off with their boasts, seeing the worth of their stories fall into the place of lies. It was this, Harry would say:

There was nothing coming up against anything else. Even the building, Harry would say, the everyday unfolding of the secret of the pipe, had somehow lost some of what made the work worth doing. They all had begun the same way they had always begun—Harry's father working the machines and heavy skill tools, Harry's mother holding boards, taking measurements, and keeping the site in plenty of iced tea, while Mr. Oates did what he did in the way of overseeing, securing permits, and providing supplies they had all had the common sense not to ask after—strange odds and ends of already angle-cut lumber with spray-painted marks and stamped with countless mill names. Harry and Tom had done their part as well, setting themselves to the task of cleaning and saving, stockpiling scraps and picking up the vinyl-coated nails that at other sites were never picked up, but at that time, to them, were worth every cent of their eight- and sixteen-penny weight.

Still, Harry would say, despite the sameness in the way it began, there was an air, a smell of something gone bad. There was an air, Harry would say, that even change could not change.

Not even a new job, Harry recalled, for himself and Tom—the further task of stripping the forms, wielding the burkebar and breaking the snap ties, getting their hands at last on the tools they had always loved to just say the names of—could shake the feeling of what they felt in their bones. They could see it, Harry thought, himself and Tom, right through the size of the thing that they built as it grew up in steps, rising from ground level on this side, to taller than a house or a tree on that side, descending in fast, curving sweeps of shape that Harry had never before seen in either metal or wood, and the masses of pipe that stopped off at each level—weird knots of copper and chrome. Through it all they saw it, Harry and Tom, growing, bigger than the thing that they built, bigger than he and Tom and the rest put together, taking them over, larger than life.

They saw it most of all in Mr. Oates, who had on this project spent some time on the making of a sign, an advertisement in advance of the product—a practice he had, since clear back to Spiveyland, since all his life, considered a jinx—a sign, what Harry and Tom had come to believe had damned the place before it began, showing the name of the place painted in cool blue blocks against a palm-tree backdrop—The Mirage.

Harry and Tom could see it, Mr. Oates's falling into his own place, pushed, nearly, apart now from Harry and Tom, careful with his step, afraid, it seemed to them, guarded, almost.

But Harry and Tom and Spivey had remained faithful, Harry remembered, greeting Mr. Oates and Dog, Harry and Tom still shouting a holler when they saw coming from Jack's Ditch the dust of Harry's father. They kept their faith through the official naming of the corner and the paving of their road, and after a new house was built on the spot where the pickup had rolled over, after the dust of the dirt had completely disappeared. They kept their faith as through that summer the road became a street and filled up and grew with numbers of cars and trucks too many to count. They kept their faith as the clover continued to grow around Tom's unseeded lady, and the first grass pushed through the dirt underneath. They kept their faith as they saw the cottonwood tree begin to turn its leaves, shed its floating seed. They kept their faith, waiting on Mr. Oates, waiting on The Mirage, waiting through the silent, grinding growth of it all, waiting on what Harry guessed he and Tom even then had known was a sweetwater spring run long since dry.

They kept their faith, Harry would say—and he would begin to grin again in so saying, reminding his listener here of the tragicomedic nature of his tale—right up until the time Spivey poked her nose where it ought not to have been poked, surprised and awoke a slumbering skunk. Spivey got a snootful, a caved-in faceful, an entire dashhound body full of the best of what that skunk could cut loose with.

"Oh, it was bad, all right," Harry would say, and clap his hands, giving the Dutch rub to the white-haired flat of his old dog's muzzle. "But one thing—it made a person stand up and take stock."

What it made Harry and Tom do was to run. They ran from Spivey, Harry and Tom—who wouldn't?—and Spivey, in need of love and affection to soothe her wounds, chased after. Down through the gullies and up through where the onions grew wild, to the place where the now-paved road joined into the top of the hill where their bikes had been left, Spivey chased after Harry and Tom, her hill-hardened paw pads striking sparks off the hot black asphalt. Spivey chased the two all the way down to Harry's house, where Harry and Tom ditched their bikes and sprinted on up the crushed-gravel drive, past the fence and the yard and Tom's naked lady, past where neither had stopped to bother or fix the rolling truck sprinkler that had come off its track, flooding the dirt underneath to mud.

Harry was the first to hit the door and discover the lock, shouting, "Shit!" Tom answering, "Shit!" the both of them shouting, "Shit! Shit! Shit!" while Spivey, panting and teary-eyed, jumped at their bare legs, pleading for a pet. Harry and Tom raced then around the house to check the windows, neither quite tall enough to see all the way in, Harry finally riding Tom's shoulders, checking first the living room, next the kitchen, last the bedroom.

"Jesus Christ!" Harry had said. "They're there! Let me down!"

"Let me up," Tom said, "let me see!"

But Harry would not let Tom up, partly because they really had been there, his mother and Mr. Oates, but mostly, Harry could now say with some humor, because Mr. Oates unspruced was for a fact not a thing you would want even your forever best friend to see with your mother.

Harry and Tom ran instead down to Mr. Oates's one-ton Ford—passing again the scaled-down version come off its track, turning the mud now into a lake—and clambered all hands and knees to the top of the flatbed planks with Dog, where soon they learned that in all the times of Spivey's misspent efforts it had been a skunk-sprayed dog Dog had sought, Dog going wild for Spivey on the ground, Dog skittering back and forth at the edge of the truck bed, then throwing good sense after bad and doing it— jumping—hanging himself at the end of his rope, tongue-

lolled and eye-popped, Spivey in a shark-feeding frenzy—
she had never been so close—Harry going after the pick
to chop Dog free.

Dog got free, and it was Spivey's turn to take to her
heels, retreating to the house, leaving Harry and Tom atop
Mr. Oates's pickup, slack-jawed and speechless, until from
behind the house, where Harry and Tom could not see,
there came a shriek more human than dog, but which Harry
and Tom both knew was Spivey—Spivey who had never
shrieked like that, not even when the vet had pulled the
quills out through her mouth what seemed like so long a
time ago. And then there reappeared Dog, bounding por-
poiselike down toward the yard, arcing up and down as
he moved forward in lurches, awkward, disjointed, snow-
bound bounds, caused by Spivey, Harry and Tom could
now see, Spivey underneath Dog, between Dog, shrieking
and stuck.

In a whisper, Harry said, "Oh, fuck."

In a whisper, Tom said, "No shit."

But they were froze, the two of them, Harry would say,
froze to the flatbed part of Mr. Oates's one-ton Ford as
Dog took Spivey crashing through the chicken-wire fence,
dragging her through the mud, tumbling and tearing up
the turf, spreading the seed through Tom's naked lady. Mr.
Oates and Harry's mother came out next, Harry's mother
just as slack-jawed and speechless as Harry and Tom, Mr.
Oates the only one among them to have had head enough
to go straight for the hose, and to chase and turn the cold
water on Dog and Spivey until the two came unstuck, Dog
once again beating his tail-tucked ass back up to where he
was safe.

Harry and Tom watched, saw Harry's mother approach Mr. Oates, pause at his side. It got quiet in a hurry, Harry remembered, putting him at the time strangely in mind of the fizzing up and down of a Coca-Cola, or else of a telegram announcing the death in a part of the family none of them had ever really known. There were no more shrieks from Spivey, no howls from Dog, not a word between any of the human-being types. They just stood there, Harry remembered, Mr. Oates and Harry's mother, stood where Harry and Tom could see Spivey lying still, flopped in the mud with what had looked surprisingly to them like a smile spread out on those teeth shown slightly off of center from the crown of her dashhound head.

"Mr. Oates left," Harry would each time wind up by saying, and he would take the corner slow, careful to keep an eye out on his own gray-snouted dog, riding now the way he always rode, standing tall on top of the tool box mounted across the back of Harry's half-ton pickup. "Mr. Oates couldn't get out of there fast enough. We all watched him. We watched until Mr. Oates was so far down the road that without the dust he could have been anybody else." Harry would get out of his pickup, walk over to where his dog stepped into his arms to be set down on the ground. "Turned out it was the last we saw of Mr. Oates. We never finished The Mirage. Mr. Oates got his permit revoked on account of that year's drought and population growth. My mother," Harry would say, "never did talk about it, didn't even remark it when later we all saw the trees he'd brought weren't Lombardys at all, but Spanish olive and willows—trash trees, really." Harry would rap the top of his old dog's head with his balled-up knuckles, lift the animal's chin with the flat of his hand. "Spivey died while birthing," Harry would say, "and I got this one here. You can bet I never named him." Harry would watch the dog's blinking eyes slow until they closed one last time and the animal was asleep on his feet. "This town has changed," Harry would say. "But don't you worry. This dog of mine might not be much to look at now, but he was a stud in his day. And I'm a builder," Harry would say. "No, sir, don't you worry. I love this dog. I love this town. No, ma'am. You might not think it to look at me, and you might not believe it to see me in action, but I'll tell you, sir, I am full of it, folks—I am full of love."

Bombardiers

THE OLD MAN, looked to Harry like, was drunk. Looked to Harry like the old man had been drinking, maybe, since noon. Maybe drinking all day. Maybe sixty years. Maybe all his life. This old man, looked to Harry like, was pickled in the fucking stuff. Preserved in it. This old man, Harry thought, was flammable.

Harry tapped the bar top with his wallet, ordered a pack of cigarettes and a Coors, paid with his last five-dollar bill. He shook out a cigarette, lit it.

This old man, the drunk, Harry saw, was heading on to him. Harry watched the old man crossing the casino, touching the chair backs of the blackjack players as he came. Harry saw the blackjack players turn their heads. When the old man had come near enough, Harry made out the name stitched onto the old man's janitor's jumpsuit.

Ed.

Harry squinted one eye against his cigarette smoke, kept the other eye on Ed.

Ed saw Harry watching, smiled with his lips. Then this

old man, this Ed, looked to the empty stool next to Harry and made a signal with his eyebrows.

Caught, Harry shrugged—and swiveled on his stool, scooped his cigarettes and change up off the bar top, slipped it all into his coat pocket.

"Mind?" Ed said.

Harry could smell the old guy.

A cocktail waitress passed by carrying a tray of drinks out to the scattered gamblers.

Harry leaned after the woman, checking her up and down, making sure.

"Not bad, eh?" said Ed. "She's a dandy, all right," Ed said.

Harry didn't say anything. He did not turn his head. But he could feel Ed standing there, an old man, still not sitting. So Harry smoked and watched the waitress serve the gamblers. He watched the legs of the waitress. She had, Harry thought, good legs.

"Course," Ed said, "she's married. To a dealer. Most of these gals here's married. Cocktail gals, that is. Mostly to dealers. Or else to bartenders. Never see a cocktail gal married to a change jockey, or to a cook, is what I mean. It's what I'm trying to say," Ed said. "To tell you."

Harry drank.

After a time, he turned to see what Ed was up to, why the man wasn't sitting. Harry saw him, Ed, standing there, patting all his uniform pockets with his palms. Harry saw Ed patting first the pockets at his chest, next the pockets on his legs, then the pockets behind. Then Harry saw him start all over again, this patting.

"That one there, though," he was saying, "Sue's her name, she's a dandy. Yessir," he said. "Like I say, she'll talk to a guy."

Harry put out his cigarette. He studied Ed's face while he put out his cigarette. Ed kept pushing his lips way out and then relaxing them, letting them hang into his chin and jowls all fleshylike, except not fatlike, but more, to Harry, rubberylike. And his skin, Harry saw, was hardly wrinkled or marked in any way, and was pink, and smooth, and was a way Harry would never have expected it to be. It was the smoothest, rubberiest face Harry had ever seen on an old man ever.

He put his bottle down between his legs. He ran his finger through his ear, inspected what came from there. He picked his bottle up. From the corner of his eye he could still see Ed working his face and patting his pockets. Then Ed stopped patting and pulled out from one of his leg pockets a stack of drink tokes. From his chest pocket he took out a pack of cigarettes. He fished around in his other leg pocket and found a lighter.

He put these things on the bar and sat down.

Harry marked all this carefully. He marked about twenty drink tokes, half a pack of cigarettes, the kind of funny old Zippo lighter certain guys go crazy over.

He finished his beer, set the empty next to Ed's things.

HARRY HAD SWITCHED to the hard stuff.

"Whatever you're pouring," he had told the bartender, then said, "no, make it Bushmills."

"Hell, yes," Ed had said. "Might as well make it two. It's all on the house," and Ed gave the bartender two of the drink tokes.

Ed did this three times, and as Harry sipped the top off the third little glass, he reckoned that made the old man good for seven more rounds, reckoned, too, that if Ed could stay upright on his stool, and that if he, Harry, had the stomach for it, they would be in cigarettes for every one of those rounds. Ed's cigarettes.

Ed offered another cigarette. Harry noticed the shake in Ed's hand. Ed held out the lighter. Harry lit the cigarette and smelled the lighter-fluid smell. On the lighter he saw there was painted some kind of old plane against a pair of crossed lightning bolts.

"So what'd you say your name was again?" Ed was saying.

"Drake," said Harry. "Still Drake."

Ed moved his eyes back and forth in his rubbery face. The old guy's eyes, Harry saw, were wet. He did the thing with his lips.

"Don't believe I know any Drakes," said Ed.

Harry gave his attention back to the casino. It had gotten crowded. Music had started up from over at the cabaret. Slots and video poker machines made video machine sounds. A croupier called out a winner, and a whoop went up from a lively craps game. Harry figured it was around midnight.

He sipped his Bushmills. He felt Ed sipping, too.

He felt Ed thinking.

Ed said, "Did know a fella once, called himself Drakos.

Hell of a name, that. Did you ever hear such a name? Course, he said it Drakos, like in Dracula, where you say yours Drake, like in rake."

Harry set his elbows on his knees. He watched the ash grow on his cigarette. But did not turn to tip it into the tray. Instead, he closed his eyes and, without looking, he tipped the ash onto the carpet.

"Greek fella, he was," said Ed, "this Drakos. Used to work out in the old man's hanger, before the old man died, that is, and the hotel took over this place."

Harry took himself a big swallow from the little glass. He swirled the ice cubes. The machines and the callers, the laughter and the music—all got louder to him. Ed's voice got louder to him.

"Was a different place then," Ed was saying, "than what you see here now. These blue shirts on the dealers, dollar tables on a Saturday night, and this music piped all around the house; never see that when the old man ran the place. No, sir," Ed said, "was a classy place then. Strictly black-and-white. Very quiet, no dollar-table riffraff. Made a guy feel good to work here. Made a guy feel like somebody, working here," he said.

On the floor, Harry spotted the waitress Ed called Sue. He wondered was her name really Sue, and was she really married.

"But back then," Ed was saying, "I really was somebody. Was a flyer. It's how I used to know that fella Drakos, on account of my being a flyer. Flew for the old man. Was the only guy the old man'd let fly him," said Ed. "Only guy," he said.

Harry nodded.

The waitress, he saw, had nearly finished her round. She stopped at a table, touched a man on the shoulder. The man turned and grinned. Harry thought he saw the man try to look down her top as she bent to set his drink on the table. The man put something on the woman's tray, and Harry saw her hike up her panty hose, tug down her skirt. He drained his drink, the ice coming up against his lip, gave a quick glance over at Ed. Then smacked his empty glass down on the bar top.

"Well, hell!" Harry said. He said, "Whaddya say, Ed?"

Ed didn't say anything, but just stared out over the casino floor. Harry followed where his eyes were staring. But there was nothing that he could see. He waved his hand in front of Ed. Ed didn't flinch. His eyes, Harry saw, were still wet, only cloudy now, and he was working his lips, only slower. Harry considered the old man.

Then he straightened up on his stool and raised his voice. He asked did the cat have Ed's tongue, or was he three sheets to the wind, or else maybe was he one brick shy.

"Flyin, Ed," said Harry. "You said you flew the old man around," he said.

Out of the blue, Ed stood up, rubbed at his eyes, patted his pockets.

"Hoo, boy!" he said, "Gotta piss!"

AT FIRST Harry sat tight, heel-hooked there on the stool, staring there at his shoes, trying to make something of it.

He caught himself pushing his lips out.

He swiveled the stool around, counted out seven of Ed's

drink tokes, three of his cigarettes, and slipped these things of Ed's into his coat pocket. Twice, Harry picked up the lighter and set it back down before deciding no. Then he ground out Ed's smoldering butt, drank the old man's drink, and stood up to go.

Falling in the Holiday Season

SPOONS WAS what it was. Why spoons? He couldn't say, quite. Whenever if Harry tried to tell it—and he did try, it was no secret, "No big deal," he would say when he tried—he could never get it just right, why spoons, and he could see it in the face of whoever it was he was trying to tell—"You are not making any sense," he saw—and more, he could feel it, the not-quite-getting-it-right, just above his belt, churning, working inside, a heavyweight, trapped, on the ropes, swinging up to the body, to the chest, the head, the mouth, fighting to punch its way finally out.

It could have been anything else—anything else, that night, would have made more sense. Could have been the tree, the lights on the tree, or candy canes or mistletoe. Snow, could have been. Could have been any single item of it, what a person might pick from the eve of that day, never what it is supposed to be, never *able* to be what it is supposed to be.

But it was not any of that lot at all, Harry would say,

but spoons. Not a knife. Not a fork. Nothing pointed. Nothing sharp. Nothing to cut or to stab with—but a spoon, a pair of spoons. Dull, rounded, dipping, scooping: the damnedest thing, these spoons.

Could have been, Harry would say, maybe even Bing Crosby, crooning.

"How long," his mother had said, "since your mother has lived here?"

"Don't know," said Harry. "Too long," he said.

"I'll tell you exactly how long," his mother said. "Three years, six months, and fifteen days. That's how long."

They were carving pumpkins, Harry and his mother. On the front porch, over newspapers, they cut the tops, dug and scraped the guts, saving out the seeds to eat.

"It's cold," Harry said. "These guts are cold on your hands. I don't remember it ever being so cold."

Harry watched his mother form her lips to blow, tilting her head this way and that, until he could see it, clouding in the blue-sky sun, her breath breathed out.

She said, "Maybe I'll build a fire tonight."

His mother began again to scrape, and Harry scraped, too, hearing the pumpkin's hollow-walled sound, smelling the orange of the pumpkin and of the leaves on the ground.

His mother said, "We'll salt these seeds and roast them on the fire. It's nicer on the fire than in the oven. Would you like a fire?" she said.

Harry was sixteen, maybe seventeen then.

"Sure," Harry said. "A fire would be great."

In a side-eyed glance he saw his mother reach, then backhand a strand of hair off her forehead, the pumpkin slick and inky on her fingers. Harry stared at her hands, crab-red under the ink, resting now on the lip of the hole of the pumpkin, her gut-slick fingers tapping the tips of her thumbs, moving from finger to finger and back.

His mother, he saw, not one week home, had pasted to her face a face like somebody's smile-idea—bared teeth, upturned lips. His mother said, "I have not built a fire since I don't know when. Wouldn't a fire be nice tonight?"

Harry held his pumpkin high in front of himself, turned it around and around, sizing it up. He could feel his mother's eyes not on him. This would be a mean pumpkin, Harry thought. This would be a very scary pumpkin. This pumpkin would keep them in candy till Christmas. This pumpkin, Harry thought, would be a bad-ass motherfuck.

Harry stood, placed the pumpkin on the porch rail.

"So what will it be?" his mother said.

"Not sure yet," Harry said.

Harry sat, began with the felt-tip pen to draw it out. His mother kept on scraping, digging hard at the hollow walls.

Coming from on the breeze, Harry could smell smoke, saw his mother quit scraping, look down the lane toward where the smoke was coming from.

"Is that the Kralls," Harry's mother said, "still burning leaves? Seems like they're always burning something."

Harry stayed seated, did not answer his mother or even move to notice until he had put the last thin line at the corner of his pumpkin's eye—a slit.

His mother stood, worked her crab-red hands, rubbing them into each other, the pumpkin guts going dry, newspaper-black, making her fingers stick.

"It's getting dark," his mother said. "Does your father always, always come home after dark?"

Harry saw his mother's nostrils, red-rimmed, flex. She had promised this time to stay off it, to not go near it, not to touch a drop.

Harry reached for the knife.

His mother leaned her weight against the porch rail. His mother said, "Was she nice, this girl?"

Harry plunged the knife, heard the sucking thunk.

ABOUT THE PUMPKINS, one thing Harry nearly almost always forgot to tell, was what his father said when, coming home not until the next day after and pointing at the one pumpkin, the round-eyed, bright-eyed, and smiling one, which one you could see clear through to the candle giving light inside, flickering, glowing, blowing out at the slightest hint of wind, about this pumpkin his father said, "That one there looks like a real dope."

NOVEMBER, Harry remembered, Thanksgiving, had passed, the three of them, himself, his mother, and his father, sitting around the company table, china-spread, silver-laid, holding hands, his father to lead the once-in-a-year Thanksgiving grace, blessing the Lord for these, His gifts: steaming, buttered green beans and a ten-pound turkey, stuffed, white meat for his mother, dark meat for his father, some of each meat for Harry, and potatoes, mashed and beaten, whipped stiff, and sugared yams and shake-thick gravy, aspic, and rolls, mincemeat pie, coffee, and

wine, nine glasses for his father, four for Harry, ginger ale
for his mother, who served, the way she had always served,
in a stand-up, sit-down, worried sort of way, holding bowls
and platters with wrung-out, work-worn hands, dishing,
reaching, always asking, "Is it enough? Do you like it? Is
it good? There's more, plenty more where that came from,"
the way the girl had never asked or served, long-legged,
lacquer-nailed, was never meant to serve but to be served,
smarter, that way, to Harry's mind, than his mother, who
every year, except those three years, served up all of what
took her two days of hard kitchen labor to make, all of
what took Harry and his father, after football, a heartbeat
to eat, a day to digest, a year to wait until the next Thanksgiving feast, three hundred sixty-five dinners to be eaten
off the anyday table, then to pass away into graceless
nights.

SHE GAVE UP cigarettes. It was another easy thing to forget,
in the middle of what all else that happened, his mother's
giving up cigarettes, but she did it, Harry would say, just
like that.

"Give me that thing," his father had said.

His mother gave his father the cigarette. His father
pressed a button on the remote control and the TV news
went mute. Harry watched his father. He watched his
mother. He watched them both, saw his father breathe in,
saw his father breathe out the gray-smelling smoke. Harry
saw his mother do what she did, tapping thumbs to fin-
gertips, finger to finger and back. Harry could see, too, the
TV newsman, whose mouth moved fast now and with no

sound coming out. His father pointed the cigarette at his mother.

"Okay," his father said. "Okay," he said, and pulled from his shirt pocket a soiled knot of nose rag. His father took a drag from the cigarette, a long, cheek-denting, chest-puffing pull, then held the rag up and blew—hard.

"See that?" his father said.

Harry saw his mother, licking at her lips, lean toward his father, look into the rag.

"That's your lungs," his father said. "That's your teeth and breath," he said. "That's your lousy yellow finger-nails."

His father stubbed the butt, pressed a button on the box so the newsman talked.

His father said, "This is your mother," and tossed the rag into Harry's lap.

CUTTHROAT SEASON! It got to be December, cutthroat season. Harry's father had only not come home once in that Thanksgiving time between the cutthroat season, and his mother had stuck to her guns, keeping to her meetings. What Harry's father had done, to make sure, was to mark the bottles. What Harry's mother had done, to make double sure, was to hang sticker reminders about the house—EASY DOES IT, ONE DAY AT A TIME. It had not been all bad, not bad at all, all things considered.

But forget all that, Harry would say. Forget *not bad*. Forget the turkey-bird sandwiches—cranberry, cream cheese, and mayonnaise. Forget the bone-boiled, turkey-souped carcass—onion and pepper, celery and carrots.

Turkey enchiladas? Baked cheddar, pimientos, and corn tortillas? No way! Skip it! Do not even think about it, Harry would say.

Cutthroat season!

Think about winter, he would say, real winter, in the desert, the northern desert. Think about mile-high valleys and eight-, nine-, ten-thousand-foot peaks. Think in blocks. Big blocks. Blocks of blue, white, brown, and black. Call them sky, snow, earth, and tree. Think in swaths, bands —up to down, down to up. Keep it simple, hard-edged, and sharp. Now see the wind whip the ridge, way up on the cornice, wisping tailings sailing white into blue, blue into white; see the wind blow down, white band to black, black to brown, windswept hills spilling down to neighborhood houses, Harry's neighborhood, Harry's house, where Harry stood, not seeing it, he would say, because of the dark, but feeling it, because he knew it, in his nose, in his skin, could know the blowing waves of sage, know the needle prick of Jeffrey pine and the underfoot crunch of hard-frozen snow, and the blue-ice cheek sting of winter-hued sky, could know it all on the wind from where he worked in the drive, loading the boat to go, hurrying there, all of them there, routinely there, there under the high morning stars, the cold winking lid over it all.

THERE WAS a fog on the lake. There was none of what Harry had expected. But better. The best, he would say. What better, Harry would say, than himself sat sitting in the middle, his father at the bow, his mother at the stern, outboard trolling in the silver-sided skiff, lines paid out, waiting for the heavy strike and the sudden queer dead of the cutthroat come up from the summer deep, while all the while needing nothing more than to watch for the sun he knew would come from across the lake under the un-fogged half?

His father, Harry remembered, worked the rudder and the throttle, keeping the speed constant, sticking near the pyramid, careful not to go too far into the fog, careful, too, not to come up onto the rocks.

His mother, Harry remembered, gloveless, hands already gone that crab-red color, lit matches, her fingers seeming brittle as the sticks, striking one match after the other, trying to get the little white-gas stove to light.

Nobody spoke. Nobody ever spoke, and on that day the steady splutter and chug of the outboard motor, the curling blue haze of burnt gas passing into the hang of fog, made it sound to Harry quieter than silent.

His father steered nearer the pyramid.

His mother got the stove lit.

From under the fog, on the face of the lake, Harry could see the clean line that split shadow and light come closer.

His father bumped up the idle, steered back off the rocks. His mother poured the water, stirred what was in the mugs.

Harry listened, felt in his seat where he sat the lap and lick of the still water on the silver-sided skiff. He listened, felt the outboard motor buzz behind his eyes. In the quieter-than-silent, he felt the fog slip by the slide of rock that was the pyramid, disappearing down into the lake, up into the sky. He listened, felt in the flesh on his bones the sun burn closer.

From his mother's outstretched hand Harry took the mug. From his father's hand he took the bottle. He sipped from the mug, the warmth and the heat of the drink mixing in his chest.

Harry narrowed his eyes, followed the ribboning slant of each of their lines. Harry leaned over the water, saw his face made larger in the mirror of the lake. He and his father, Harry remembered, had fished the surface, using the lightweight woolly-worm lures. His mother, he remembered, had fished the deep, using a heavier lure, a diver, a three-hook, flat-back spoon.

WHY THE CAN? Harry would say. Why did she have to use that can? Okay, he would say, sure, she could not just stand up and aim it over the side the way they had stood up and aimed it over the side. But why didn't she at least sort of try to hang it out? Or, better, why not hold it? Didn't she know how that sounded, in that can, that racket? Didn't she know the girl would never ever in a hundred thousand years ever use that can?

THE WAY HARRY caught her—and it was the hardest part for him to tell—was on her knees, rump up, nose down to the sheet-stripped bed. But she never stopped doing what she was doing there on the sheet-stripped bed, even after Harry could see she knew she was caught, but kept right at it, nosing over every inch of it.

When at last she had quit, and had got off the bed,

and was standing fixing up her hair in front of the mirror, Harry did not leave the room the way he thought he had wanted to, but stayed, sat himself on the edge of that bed. Harry watched from the edge of the bed, saw his mother comb her hair, stick pins in it, clip the smoke-streaked strands back tight against her head.

His mother said, "What do you think of your mother?"

Harry leaned back, propped himself up on his elbows.

He saw his mother begin to open and close the drawers, pushing her hands through the things in the drawers, holding some of the things up to her nose, pausing then, though never stopping until the last drawer had been opened and closed.

His mother moved to the closet.

His mother said, "Do you love your mother, Harry?"

Harry lay all the way back on his back.

He could hear his mother there in the closet, the shifting and sliding of hangers, the metal-on-metal scrape. Harry closed his eyes, covered his eyes with his arm, heard the scraping stop.

"Harry," his mother said. "Harry," she said, "don't kid yourself, honey."

Harry heard the cap of the bottle come off, heard the cap of the bottle go back on.

His mother's weight laid down next to him on the bed. He could feel his mother's fingers moving on the sheet-stripped mattress. He could hear her tongue wet on her lips. He could smell the stuff sweet on his mother's breath as she breathed so near.

His mother had been home not three months.

"Harry," his mother said. "It gets lonely, Harry, being alone."

THERE WAS SNOW, he would say, six days old, and the light-strung, tinsel-hung tree, the record his mother had played, the fire she had built, and the smell of the just-done stuffing coming from the kitchen.

There was all of that and there was not his father, who had started to not come home almost every other night, and there was Harry, pumping the pedals of the exercise bike, a present given early, his father to his mother, to help her to lose the weight she had gained since quitting the smoking, his father since seen noting her pounds on the scales, scribbling his mother's numbers in pencil on the pad, adding, subtracting, pleased, it seemed to Harry, Harry seeing nothing better or worse but only his mother, who stepped off the scales, the somebody's smile-idea pasted to her face, to make her way out to the kitchen, there to bake the cookies and candies for the Christmas season, to start to end up her first holidays back with her family at home.

It was hot, Harry remembered, pumping the pedals like that—so near his mother's fire—when his father got back from where he had been and kissed his mother there in the kitchen where Harry could see. Harry kept pumping, shifted gears, pumped harder, got hotter, and what he got next he never could say—whether if it was the heat and the sweat, the friction whir and whine of the wheel spinning circles, or the sight of his mother stuffing the stuffing, her hands filling the hollow of the bird's emptied middle, or if maybe it was one of those little things inside grown big, too big, that made him not want to hear his father saying to get off that bike, to quit, to stop.

Whichever it was that did it, it got him jerked off that bike, sat down on the couch, where his father's finger came as a stiff, steady jab to Harry's fast-pounding chest. Whichever it was that did it, it got himself back up to knock his father down, sticking his head to his father's ribs, for that one shocked second Harry falling up top, then, just as fast, his father muscling back over and up, then, almost as fast, his father getting off and letting both of them up. They came up, Harry and his father, facing each other, and stood standing there, neither speaking, catching their breath.

It felt good to Harry, standing like that. He could have screamed a hole through the ceiling, it felt so good.

WHENEVER if Harry told it, he would tell all he knew there was to tell. Seated, he would rock, back and forth and back, his hands in his lap, his fingers locked one into the other to the thumb.

Harry left his father, went to his mother, where in the kitchen he saw how the bird had been dropped, the stuffing knocked out from the middle. Harry saw the thin line of his mother's lips pressed tight, her hands in a chalk-white clutch around the anyday spoons. Harry took the spoons from her chalk-white hands. He held the spoons high in front of his face and under the light, turning them over and back. Harry brought the spoons up close to his lips, his breath a fog on the cool surface mirror—and when the fog had cleared, and the shine had spread, there was left only himself that he could see, his mouth there, his teeth, his upturned lips turned upside down, his whole face a thing grown small on the spoon's inward-curving silver slope.

The Naming

WHAT WAS her name? Didn't matter to him, names. But it had to her.

"Oooo, sick!" she had squealed. "It's so hairy! That's exactly what I'm going to call it—*Harry*, Harry!"

And it was so hard, and big, he thought, for a kid's, and crooked, after all, and looking, along with the rest of what else was there, like a ripe, yellow squash. It felt so hard and crooked there, he thought, that all the summer's water going down that cold, cold ditch couldn't put a dent in it.

He said, "Your turn now."

She made a face and pulled up her T-shirt. He got an eyeful and saw she was getting them, all right, both of them, only it was funny because in the short time before she jerked her shirt back down, he could have sworn the one was bigger than the other.

But that was how it had been with her.

.   .   .

HARRY KNEW she was nothing hot to look at. He knew she was no great shakes. He knew, even then, she was the kind of girl who would be the kind of woman who wouldn't use perfume, whose face would show whiskers in the frost, whose pants would be baggy in the butt, whose legs would be bristly on your back.

But none of that mattered to Harry.

What mattered to him was this: she was who she was and she was, in the end, a girl, who, somehow or other— by love or by money, by hook or by crook—could get him to do things he would not do.

While her shirt was up, he reached for one, the big one, then changed his mind.

ONE OF THE THINGS she got him to do was to sing.

"Sierra Boys Choir?" said Harry.

"Think of it this way," she said, "think of it as training. You are training your voice to be a rock-and-roll singer. Picture yourself on TV," she said. She said, "In leather pants, how about?"

Rehearsals went once a week, three hours a shot. Harry was an alto. If he stood up straight, he was taller by almost a head than the guy standing to either his left or his right, or in front or behind, taller by a head, almost, than nearly the whole crowd of them. He almost always stood up straight. They sang things like "They Call the Wind Maria," and "The Hills Are Alive." They sang in bits and pieces, stopping and going, repeating things, changing things, trying to improve things to the point where they might once slip the whole lousy song by the chorus master standing there waving his arms around, holding his one blue-veined hand from time to time to his skinny ear, saying things like "What? What's this I hear? Fifth bar, second measure, please!" and on this one day coming closer to them, stopping right in front of where Harry was, tilting his head, putting his hand to his ear, then looking straight at Harry, cutting off the singing, and saying, "You are thirteen years old, Mr. Drake. You are an alto. One day, maybe tomorrow, you will wake and find yourself a tenor, maybe even a bass."

Harry heard one of the sopranos giggle.

"But for now you are an alto," the chorus master continued, "and I suggest you don't hurt yourself straining to sing the notes you cannot yet reach."

SHE WAS WAITING for him outside the church. He saw her hair oil-slick in the sun.

She said, "How'd it go?"

He got his bike unlocked, mounted up. They took off. The bike breeze felt fresh on his face.

"Sissies!" Harry shouted. "Faggots and fairies!" he shouted. "Wimps!" he shouted. "Sissies and faggots and wimps!"

They rode hard up to the top of the hill. They stopped there, at the place where the pavement ended, catching their breath, airing their T-shirts.

She said, "I got cigarettes."

. . .

"ON YOUR BELLY," he said.

"What?" she said.

"On your belly, like a snake."

"I'm not getting on my belly."

"Look," he said, "I shouldn't of even showed you this. I swore I'd never show this to anybody else. But here we are, and if you want to see it, then that's what you've got to do."

They were on their hands and knees, peering down the dark hole that tunneled deep into the bottom of the blackberry thicket. He looked at her. He heard the ditch going behind, smelled the dry, bright, crushed-sage smell.

"You call it the Heart?" she said.

"That's right," he said. "Because that's what it is."

She moved closer, stuck her head part way in.

"You go first," she said.

"No way," he said. "You might get scared."

"I won't get scared."

"You might," said Harry, "and then you'd get yourself cut up pretty good trying to back out."

He saw her focus on the thorns, then squint into the dark, trying to see clear down to the Heart.

Still squinting, she said, "What difference does it make, going frontwards or backwards?"

He goosed her a good one. She jumped out of her skin. She hit him on the arm.

"So?" she said. "What difference?"

He said, "Did you ever see a snake could go backwards?"

. . .

ONE TIME, to see what would happen, she suggested they go three or four days eating nearly nothing but carrots. Carrots! They did it, the two of them, Harry couldn't believe it, then they showed each other what happened. It was pretty much the same, but it wasn't pretty.

HARRY READ THIS:

> *Gloria in excelsis Deo*
> *Et in terra pax hominibus*
> *Propter magnam gloriam*
> *Cum Sancto Spiritu*

Vivaldi's *Gloria*, he read. What did it all mean? What exactly? He never looked. He never wondered. For an hour and a half of the three hours they practiced reading these words, speaking these words, Latin words, words, the chorus master explained, nobody used nowadays, even priests in the masses—"Go sometime and you'll see," he said— didn't use these words. It was, the chorus master explained, a dead language.

"But pronounce them correctly," the chorus master said, "and sing them well, and you will feel these words come alive in your hearts; sing these words well and sing them with joy," he said, "and you will hear angels in your ears; you will hear God."

Harry wasn't sure how much of all this he could swallow.

But then the chorus master did a funny thing: he played the entire *Gloria* recording from start to finish without stopping—twice, loud—and the words and the voices, the music, music like Harry had never heard, music that felt to him like the air in the early morning, or like running, leaping down the gully and over the sage, or else swinging, swinging from the cottonwood limb, out and out over the swift-running ditch, and letting go of the rubber tire, and flying, for that moment, flying, in air—he had wings now!—weightless out and down and into the water, ice-feeling, breath-taking, free-floating water, filled the church, and when the music quit, when the church was quiet, Harry looked at the score in his hands, the bars and measures, the notes and signs, the Latin, and he asked himself who in the world would want to know, exactly, what these words meant?

LIZARDS, THEY CAUGHT. Piles of lizards. Lizards on lizards on lizards. Old tin buckets full of lizards they caught.

"Look!" she screamed. "Look! A yellow-belly!"

She pinched the thing by its head and middle, and its legs and tail clawed and whipped while she held it up for him to see. Harry set the BB gun down on the flat granite rocks. He stroked the fast-breathing, soft-shining under scales.

"That's not a yellow-belly," he said. "It's blue."

"Well," she said, "to me it's yellow."

She started to put the lizard in the bucket.

"Wait!" he said. "Let me take one more look," Harry said, and grabbed her wrist, and broke the tail off.

.   .   .

Sixty-two lizards, Harry figured, more or less, they caught that day, and twelve horned toads, and the two-foot bull snake—all of what they hauled up nail-scratching and live-fighting in the old tin bucket out of the trickle-creek gully, and to the top of the hill where the tree house and ditch were—where they tipped the whole scattering mess free, and watched. Then Harry raised his BB gun, aimed it at a lizard that had stopped to do what looked like push-ups on a rock.

But the lizard disappeared from the rock.

She said, "Don't you ever do that again."

He remembered he never did.

Each time now the chorus master played that Vivaldi *Gloria* straight through, and he had them sing it that way, too. He told them that the alto and soprano parts were sung by the Westminster Cathedral Boys Choir, from England. He told them that they, the Sierra Boys Choir, sounded every bit as good. He told them that they, the Sierra Boys Choir, would be performing the Vivaldi *Gloria* along with the University Choir and the Reno Philharmonic in September, at the Pioneer Theatre Auditorium.

Right there in his face, never more than a knife's length separating, never more than a fork's length apart, close enough to sip with a straw, close enough to dish with a spoon—the soles of her shoes was all, in front, he saw. On the sides and above, all around and pressing close down on them, was the blackberry thicket, where this time of year no berries yet grew, but where leaves were, and the thorns, and the wet, early summer smell of things sprouting from the dirt.

Harry pulled himself down the tunnel, using his elbows, walking himself, dragging himself, humping his back and flattening into and along the ground after her. He listened to her breathing and grunting and shoescraping her way down the slope. From her body's distance, he heard her curse the stickers, working, sweating.

"How much farther?" she said.

"Pretty soon, seems like," he said. "Can you see any light down there?"

"Maybe," she said.

But she had not. Instead, it got darker. He didn't remember it ever being quite so dark, or so far. He didn't remember it being quite so hard.

"Maybe it grew in," he said.

"Harry!" she said.

They kept on and his elbows felt raw and dirt got into his elastic and ground against his belly and he caught himself beginning to wonder.

"I think I see it!" she said then, and he heard her elbows working faster, saw her shoes pull away from him.

"Careful!" he said. "Not so fast. Whatever you do," he said, "don't turn left when you get in. Roll to your right."

He saw her stop dead.

"Why?"

"Just watch out," he whispered. "All right? Watch out, is all."

He felt her trying to back out, saw the toes of her shoes

flexing that way, the wrong way. Then he saw her raise to
her knees when she could not back, and he felt that, too,
because he knew it, and knew now the thorns and stickers
would be tearing her T-shirt and scratching her skin, and
so he grabbed her ankle, and he yelled.

"Stop!" he yelled. "Kidding!" he yelled. "Sorry!"

Then he saw her shoe flex back the right way, saw her
butt go down, and felt the thicket, stuck, come down, too.
He heard her taking in air. The air sounded gasping and
wet. But she never said a word.

Harry held her ankle, held it tight. He stroked her ankle.
He caressed it.

"I'm sorry," he said. "Sorry."

IN THAT SUMMER he couldn't remember hardly ever not
wearing shorts. On one pair of that summer's cutoffs,
Harry tried making it a contest to see who could split the
sides up highest. But she wasn't buying any of that.

She said, "Stupid's one thing I'm not."

They were sitting on the hill that had the onions, the hill
without the sage, across the big, now creekless, gully from
the hill that had the tree house and had the ditch and the
blackberry thicket. They were pulling the onions up. They
were wiping them off on their cutoffs and eating them.
Sometimes Harry didn't think he could eat enough of them,
these stem-green summer onions. Every so often when she
opened her mouth he caught the smell and noticed how it
was different, better, coming from her mouth instead of
from the ground.

He said, "Anyway, I wish baseball was still here."

"Why do you think they built that tree house on the hill instead of the gully?" she said.

"And school'll be starting before we know it," said Harry.

"I mean, those trees in the gully are a lot bigger," she said.

He saw her wiping the onion clean, then biting the end off with her eyeteeth.

He said, "I hate to think about it."

"Well, then I'll tell you," she said. "It's because of the view and because you can drop from the rope and into the ditch."

Harry did what she did with another onion. His lips puckered and his eyes watered. No matter how many of these onions he ate, it always happened to him like this.

INSIDE, at the bottom, in the hollow, he pulled out his pocketknife and said, "First thing—we got to mix blood."

They sat close, Indian-style, sun spotting starlike on the dark ground, the thicket branch and earth cutting off the running ditch sound. She looked at him, peered at him through the darkness. He waited. But she didn't say a word either way. Then he held his own left hand up in a shaft of light, right up where he knew she could see it, right up under her nose, and then he made the tiny incision on his finger, squeezing the finger so the blood would really come out.

She held her cut finger up where his was.

"Brothers," Harry said.

. . .

"I CAN'T," she said.

"Oh yes you can," said Harry.

"I can't," she said.

"Oh, c'mon," Harry said.

"Really, Harry. I can't."

"You can too."

"Cannot."

"Can too."

"Cannot," she said.

"Why not?" Harry said.

"Because," she said.

"Because why?" Harry said.

"Just because."

"Why because?"

"Because I can't."

"But why?"

"Because I'm too young," she said. "All right?" she said.

"You're not too young," Harry said.

"I am," she said.

"Then why'd you let me take your pants off?" Harry said.

"I don't know," she said. "Give me my pants," she said.

But he didn't give her her pants back but laid her down on the splintery plywood floor of the tree house, where he saw her close her eyes to the million insect-crawling cottonwood leaves during the kiss he tried to give her. He kissed her with his eyes closed, too, the way he thought you were supposed to kiss them. They kissed hard, with the mosquitoes buzzing around their heads and the birds squawking and the spiders screaming and the grass shrieking. They kissed hard and they probably wouldn't have heard any of it—not even the ditch running down beneath. But they did. They heard the ditch when they heard her pants jingling coins as the coins fell from the tree house and the pants fell from the tree house. They saw her pants going floating down the ditch because they stopped kissing when they heard them falling—jingle-jingle-jingle—into the ditch that ran on and on all summer every summer just as Harry's hand reached between her legs and felt something like a barnacle clinging to an old pier.

She stayed up in the tree house with the birds and the bugs while Harry went and fetched her a pair of his pants for her. She wouldn't let him come back up but made him throw the pants from where he stood on the ground. He saw her face sticking out from the edge of the plywood floor.

"You just stay down there," she said.

Harry wound up to throw.

"Old Jinglepants!" Harry shouted, and threw.

THEY HAD lockers now, past Labor Day, and combinations, and things to put in the lockers, secret things, if they wanted, and class periods, too, one through seven, and halls that filled after bells, but when it came time—Harry didn't ask her, but asked the deer-legged girl who had a locker above his, Sylvia Glass, a new girl, one he had never seen anywhere before but who smelled like everything he ever had wanted, would she please come hear him sing the *Gloria?*

HE GOT OUT from behind the wheel and ran. Down through the wild onions he ran, bounding, the soft soil sinking his feet when he hit, then blurring beneath him in leaps. He hit the gully bottom—picked, skipped, and jumped his way through the dry-creek rocks. He started up the other side. Straight up, he started, raising his knees high, running up through the brush, sucking air, on the ditch trail, at the base of the giant cottonwood tree already losing yellow leaves. He straightened, put his hand on his chest, and was amazed at the beating. He had never felt it beat like that. He tilted his head way back and looked up at the plywood bottom. But there was no sound of anything. Even the ditch, drained last week, was silent. He hollered up. He got no answer. He threw sticks and stones up there and heard the one stone clunk against the plywood and saw it not come down. Harry went up, climbing ancient two-by-fours, sixes, and eights—and he peeked, slowly, up over the floor, and saw nothing but the stone.

Change Jockey

NFOS they called them. *Niggers from Oakland.* Harry made them change, the NFOS. In yellow-threaded letters stitched against the black vest on his back it was printed: CHANGE. Each night he caught a holler on his ear and a finger on his shoulder, some colored face or other come up to ask it—change. And Harry made it, change. It was his job to make it. He paid rent, making it. White faces, yellow faces, red, brown, and black, Harry made them all, excepting the one, change.

She was an NFO, that one excepted. With a whitewashed row of picket-fence teeth and the full-moon curve of a horsewoman's rump she was to Harry's eye as fine a female prospect as a searching person might expect. She packaged it fine. She was a fine package. Harry would see her, the way she was all dolled up in a sheer slip of something clung to the curve of her horsewoman's rump, sliding her package through the midnight tables, the blackjack-playing eyes of rough men and highbrow alike raised up off the cards to see her saunter, their adam's-appled throats swallowed hard above their slack white collars. She parted her lips for those men. Harry saw her part the full-fleshed meat of her lips and show those men that whitewashed row of her picket-fence teeth.

She had, Harry knew, herself a career going here. She did not squander one ounce of her God-hung talents. It was the highbrow men Harry saw that looked longer than the rough.

But highbrow or not, Harry knew by nights of watching while paying out change that horses, picket fence, and whitewash did not play in any way in the world this sister lived in. This sister, she was an NFO, strictly a nigger from Oakland, and she had by now somehow put Harry smack in the pants he would never pick to stand in.

Harry, after all, had heard the talk. He knew the score. Harry had heard what passed as fact from the mouths of the workers in the employees lounge. He heard it from all the other change jockeys dressed just like he was dressed. He heard it from cocktail waitresses and keno runners. He heard it from the dealers. He heard it from the pit boss, even. From every race and every creed it came the same: they never tipped, the NFOs, were worse than the Canadians that way, and they got drunk, and were rude, worse than the Japanese, and, worse, worse than the Mexicans, they were crooks—hookers, pimps, and thieves, welfare panhandlers come to Reno on the Fun Bus to spend their checks and make it big on one lucky shot and no work— something, anything, for nothing.

It came the same, just like that. It never changed, and

Harry guessed he was no different than the rest, no month of Sundays passing by before he caught himself red-handed on a Saturday night wishing the Fun Bus would take out an entire load of those NFOs on a one-way plunge down the California side.

Excepting her.

Good God! Good grief!

How many nights? How many times in any single night had he stood waiting among the rows and columns of coin-clanging machines, earplugged against what he rightly pegged as Bizet's *Carmen*'s "Toreador's Song" singing out winners in that machine-bleating video voice? How many times had he moved to the edge of the rows and columns to mark her face from among the wild-eyed arrivals coming in fresh off the Fun Bus? And this: the number of times too many to count that he had turned his back to the rows and columns of women who played those machines—because it was almost mostly always women who played the machines, old women, mostly, veinated, skinny-wristed, peroxided women, women wearing plastic bags rubber-banded at their skinny wrists to cover up their bony hands, this, they would say, on account of the filth, on account of the filth, they would say, and ask Harry did he have any of those new, clean coins; could he make them spotless change, these women would ask on coming up from behind those countless times, these old machine-playing women tapping him square like that between the yellow-threaded letters to ask it again and again, and again to ask—Change? Change please? Can you make me change, boy?

Excepting her who Harry was waiting for. She never

asked for change. She never played the machines. She played the tables, Harry saw, the highbrows at the tables.

If he had a quarter, Harry thought, for every shark-eyed, zipper-headed Jap that passed in through those double doors; if he had a dime for every tight-assed Canadian hyuk-hyuk-hyukking his flat-footed way to the two-dollar tables; if he had even a lousy wooden nickel for every I-gots-the-fever shrieking NFO blowing off that fucking Fun Bus—if somebody, anybody, could spot him a stake, get Harry into the kind of game he knew she liked, he would take her: rump, teeth, and lips; breasts, legs, and belly—he would take her, every pound and inch of her, up to one of the highbrow rooms above—hook, line, and sinker Harry would take her all the way down.

Not only for that. There was that for sure, that what Harry saw was always moving just below the surface, a skin's width beneath the clinging slip of something she would always wear—something white, something red, something gold and precious seeming—and the jewelried parts, too, the glint-and-glitter rings slid down onto her fingers, the great dangled hoops pierced into her ears, and the stacked silver bracelets running up her fine-boned wrists, the pearl strand of necklace hung down to meet her breast—that, sure, yes, but more.

Harry had seen what more. Standing at his cash box while stocking up his change Harry could see the part of her he knew she would never knowingly show. He would see her there, in the corner, where the light was dim and the ceiling was low, her sitting there so still. Harry would watch, take his time changing bills back into coins, and he could see the way that nothing of her moved now, could see the way that nothing of her glinted, nothing even curved. He could see the strange, flat, rounding-out of her as she sat heel-hooked on that stool.

Harry would stock his belt then with the big silver dollars, the quarters, dimes, and nickels—feeling the weight of change there growing on his waist. He would shut the box, lock the lock, and see her press her fingers to the low place—the place someway lower than a man's—that a woman calls her belly. She would press—glintless rings on her curveless dress—her eyes then shutting closed, her lips then parting open, and she would slowly, oldly, begin to rock.

Harry watched her on the nights she came and sat and rocked like that, and he would move nearer to her, away from his box, away from the machines and the clang of the coins, and he would take out those rubber lugs that plugged his ears, and listen—straining to hear the song she rocked to. And he would hear it, sometimes, the low moaning sound that began in the belly where she pressed, a sound not made to sell, Harry guessed, but a sound already bought and paid for: the after sound, the during sound, the sound he figured the highbrows heard in the highbrow rooms so high above, sounds sometimes he, Harry, would hear, coming up from so far deep inside her, then out right between her teeth—before the old machine-playing women would come back onto him, high-pitched and hollering for change, tapping his back, tugging his sleeve, asking for coins for cash.

"Quarters!" one might say. "Got a hot one that's fixin to bust. Oh, I know it, all right. You better believe. I feel it way down here. It's a gut thing with me. Give us quarters and we'll show you. Fixin to bust, that one is."

Or this: "Say! Say, change boy! This here machine over there won't pay. Says I hit it, it does. Royal Flush on the progressive poker. I swear it to you truly. Can you come see, maybe tell me what's what over here, maybe fix it, make it pay?"

Or: "Change! Change! *Cocktails*, change!"

And Harry would make the rounds—the black vest on his back, the coin-filled belt bumping up against his legs —doing the work that paid the rent: changing out quarters for the paper bills clutched in plastic-bagged fists; and showing that no, that's a club, not a spade, you needed a spade to make that flush royal; and explaining how a person had to *play* the machines to get the drinks, they aren't really free, see? you can't just sit on that stool expecting a something for a nothing, Jack.

Each night Harry made the rounds. He heard the talk. He washed his hands. He saw the old women going over in old-women sprints to check out winners. Harry pushed the rubber plugs deeper in his ears. He breathed other people's cigarette smoke. He changed a quarter into five nickels, five pennies into one nickel. Harry saw a man go out in handcuffs. He heard the old women complain about how they had played that machine just two scant weeks ago. Harry smelled the mix of fried food and booze. He saw the old women wipe their sweating hands onto their wrinkled cotton skirts. He heard the *Carmen* "Toreador's Song" as he made his light-waisted way back to his cash box to change the bills back again into coins.

Sometimes Harry saw her, there from his cash box, her

sometimes sitting on the stool in the dim, low-ceilinged corner, rocking her rock, sounding her down-low sound, her fingers pressed into her belly.

Sometimes not.

On the not times Harry knew to look to the tables, the highbrow tables where the high-stakes chips piled up in stacks too tall to count. Not the blue-chip tables where the Canadians and her own kind played, but the tables with the black and the red and the yellow stacked chips, where the fine-suited men with the manicured hands fingered their fancy wagers on the casino-green felt, and where the well-heeled dealers were all thoroughbred beauties, and the cocktail waitresses would come around quick showing plenty of leg and orthodontic smiles.

Harry had seen her on the times he saw her, sidling up from behind the fine-suited men, leaning in close without ever touching, her pearl strand of necklace hung down into their highbrow game. Harry saw her put her face near to their faces, saw the perfume softening of the men's cheeks, eyes, and jowls. Harry saw her make her own fancy wager in her own high-stakes color, draw her cards and play her hand. Harry watched then the way she walked away, the firm-fleshed twitch and ripple of her weight always just a skin's width beneath her clinging slip. Harry saw, too, the elbows, bumps, and nudges between the men after she had left, and the glances and looks snuck from under their highbrow eyebrows that followed her over to the next high-stakes table she went to.

And sometimes Harry would see some one of those highbrow men follow her over with more than just his eyes, taking his whole highbrow self over after her to get what

Harry figured that one man would not—could not—have ever really known. That man, Harry figured, could not have known she was an NFO come up on the Fun Bus, could not have known how high the price of the deal she would strike in the rooms up above. Neither could that man have known the stiff, hair-product feel of the hair on her head, nor the pillowcase stain left the next day after. Nor never could that man have known the full-mooned curve of her rump in his palm, nor the glistening pink slit of her easy parting. Never ever, Harry figured, could that man even have imagined in a million years the strange black stink that would be his own burning urine!

But that man, Harry knew, that one man who sent himself over, paying his cash, getting the goods, would soon find out all of the parts that Harry had known more than once on this breed of girl—rump, teeth, and lips; breasts, legs, and belly—that, sure, and the part on her and her alone that was more.

Harry would watch, thought of the part of her that had been bought and paid for, the part Harry had wished and prayed for, praying since first he had seen her from there at his cash box, doing the work to make the rent, hearing again and again the call spelled out right there on the black vest he wore on his back: CHANGE.

Harry heard change. He heard losers. He heard winners. He heard Bizet's *Carmen*'s "Toreador's Song." On the bloodless lips of the bony old women and the video voice of the metal machines, Harry heard all of what the rubber lugs that plugged his ears could not keep him from hearing.

"Hey!" he heard. "Say!" he heard. "What're you deaf? I've been calling you, change boy. Can you help me please?

I've a condition, see, a female thing. Got to go upstairs to the toilet to fix it. I'll be back in a flash. Can you, change boy, please, please, please watch my machine?"

Harry would hear these old women, see their sweating hands on their wrinkled skirts, and he would do as they said so as to keep his work. At least once in each night Harry stood watch over those machines—the old women's plastic bags rubber-banded now to the one-armed knobs —this just in case—and the half-full, half-gone cups of coins, the coins in the trays, and the unclaimed credits on the video-machine screen.

Harry stood watch, watching, too, the tables, trying to keep an eye out through the rows and columns of the peroxided women, looking to see if he might see her working the highbrows, melting those men the way that she did with the way of her walk and the constant promise of things unseen and untold.

Harry would watch—hearing the tin-sounding music for bullfighting men and hot-blooded women—waiting. He began to steal, waiting. From the old women's half-full, half-gone cups Harry would take on this night maybe a scraping of quarters, on that night maybe a fistful of nickels. He might take from time to time a dollar or two from the big silver-dollar racks. Harry began as he made his rounds through the rows and columns to punch the buttons and collect the credits. He picked up dropped coins from the carpet, scooped tips from bar tops. Harry got bold, slipped bills from his cash box to his pocket. Harry got good, lifted billfolds from the old women's part way opened purses. Harry got smart, blamed the NFOs whenever the peroxided women came to him to complain.

It took time, Harry's raising the stakes that way, nickel-and-diming his way up.

How much time? Nights of time.

It had taken nights of time and the patience of a saint for Harry to get to this place to stake his claim, to shed his vest, leave his belt in that box, to follow them up, to wait his turn to take her down.

And how did it feel, trailing the two?

How many steps on those stairs?

How much higher?

Should he have waited?

Should he have left?

And what should Harry have done when at last she did show, coming out of that room alone by herself, closing the door then behind herself—the glint gone, the curve gone, her teeth now hidden behind her lips? Which way should he have finally moved, standing there with the hard green cash gripped in his coin-soiled hands, the money gotten to buy the secret, the answer one more time not what Harry would have bought, the same tired, unchanged answer weighing now on Harry's heart as low and as old as the whole world was?

Afterburners

REMEMBER ED? Old guy? Old rubbery-faced guy? Drunk-looking? Looking pickled in the stuff? Preserved in it?

"Remember me?" says Ed, and Harry lifts his chin a little to see spelled out on the old man's janitor jump-suit ED.

Cursive.

Ed.

Harry sees Ed point to himself, to the cursive printed on his chest.

"Ed?" says Ed. "Remember me?" he says.

Harry shakes his head no, he doesn't remember.

Harry looks past Ed, scanning the casino floor, and sees that they are getting past swing now, heading into grave-yard. Harry swivels back barways on his stool. He picks up his money from off the bar top, palms his cigarettes. Harry finishes his beer and signals the bartender.

"I remember you," Ed says. "Drake. Drake, like in rake—right?" he says. "Remember?"

Harry feels Ed pressing in. Ed stands in the space between

Harry's stool and the next stool over. Harry keeps his head down. He hears the old guy begin to pat himself. Up and down the pockets of his janitor's jumpsuit the old guy pats himself.

"How about this?" Ed says. "Remember this?"

Harry turns on the stool. He sees the old guy pushing his lips out and then relaxing them some. Harry thinks how even if he wanted he could never forget lips like the ones the old guy keeps pushing out of his rubbery face. But Ed doesn't mean his lips, Harry sees, but what it is that Ed pulls out from one of his pockets.

"You can't forget this," Ed says, "can you?"

It is the Zippo lighter Ed means for Harry not to forget, the one with the old airplane painted against a pair of crossed lightning bolts. Harry watches the old guy flip the lid of the lighter open and closed.

"Say," the old guy says, "I know. How'd you like to see me set my face on fire?"

Harry stares at the old guy. The old guy doesn't blink.

"Let's have a look at that thing," Harry says.

Ed holds the lighter out.

Harry reaches for the lighter.

But Ed pulls the lighter back.

"Won't forget where you got it, will you?" Ed says, and laughs.

The old guy's eyes are red and look wet to Harry.

"What do you mean by that?" Harry says.

"Not a thing, Mr. Drake," Ed says.

"Who says my name is Drake?" says Harry.

"Hoo boy!" Ed says. "That's a dandy. There's a peach for you, all right! *Who says!*"

Ed hands over the lighter. Harry examines the lighter, feels the way the old airplane and the lightning bolts are not really only just painted on the lighter but raised up off the surface some. Harry lights the lighter with his thumb and holds his hand over the flame. He flips the lid shut, puts the lighter up against his cheek.

"It's cool," he says.

"Smoke?" says Ed.

Harry slips his cigarettes into his pocket and takes the one Ed offers to him. The bartender comes back with the beer Harry has ordered. Harry makes like to find his money, but lets Ed pick the beer up with one of the drink tokes the old guy digs out from another of his jumpsuit pockets.

Ed orders for himself a Bushmills.

"For old time's sake," Ed says.

Ed takes a stool next to Harry. They sit side by side, Harry and this old guy, smoking, drinking, watching the gamblers gamble.

Ed says, "So what is your name? If it's not Drake."

"Barkey," Harry says.

"Barkey?" Ed says. "Don't believe I know any Barkeys. Got a first name?"

Harry watches the old guy monkey-lipping his cigarette. Harry says, "What's it to you?"

"Nothing," Ed says. "Sure you don't remember me?"

"I don't," Harry says. "But I'm not so good with faces."

"People change," Ed says. "I've heard that, and I believe it's true. Myself, I'm not so good with faces either."

Ed sets the lighter next to the drink tokes and cigarettes he has sitting on the bar top. Harry watches the old man's

lips work in and out and back. Harry sees the fleshy pink-
ness of Ed's cheeks.

Harry picks up the lighter, begins fooling with it.

Then Ed stops with his lips.

"Sue!" Ed says. "You'll remember Sue, sure."

Harry looks at the sogged tip of cigarette filter Ed has
pinched between his fingers. He looks at Ed's face and
decides it really doesn't look like anything so much as Ed's
face.

Harry drinks his beer.

"Can you wait?" Ed says. "She's here. Somewhere. She'll
be off soon. She works a funny sort of shift, between swing
and graveyard. But she's a looker, Sue is. She's cocktails.
You'll remember Sue," Ed says. "Can you wait till Sue gets
off shift?"

Harry helps himself to one of Ed's cigarettes.

"Okay," Harry says. "Yeah, I could wait."

THEY ARE QUIET for a while, Harry and Ed, but then Ed
begins to work his lips again, and Harry can hear the old
guy's cogs cranking up inside his rubbery head.

"Listen, Ed," Harry says, "no offense, but there's nothing new you're going to tell me tonight."

"What's it you figured I was set to say?" says Ed.

"I don't know," Harry says. "A story, right?"

"That's right," Ed says. "A story."

"Well, this is one of those nights," Harry says, "when
I could tell your story for you."

Harry reaches for another of Ed's cigarettes. He picks
up the lighter and thumbs the little ridges of the airplane.

"I get it," the old guy says. "Was a time when I was in your shoes, too, you know."

Harry watches the flame at the end of his cigarette catch, sees the smoke roll up and the white paper blacken and curl. He flips the lid of the lighter shut.

Ed says, "Was a time I flew that plane."

Harry finishes up his drink, tipping his glass high so he can see the casino lights, see the people, see the machines made wavy through the bottom. He sets the empty next to Ed's cigarettes and drink tokes, and sets the lighter there, too—then stands up as if to go.

"You wouldn't think it to look at me," Ed is saying, "but I did. Fly it, that is."

Harry makes a rough count of what is left on the bar top, tries guessing the time by the casino crowd, tries guessing which of the cocktail runners might be the one they are supposed to be waiting for.

Harry says, "I'd like to wait, Ed."

"What's that?" says Ed.

"Aren't we waiting?" Harry says.

"Sure we're waiting," the old guy says. "For Sue," he says. "Sit down. Order yourself up another snort."

Harry watches Ed's wet eyes, wet lips.

Does he have teeth? Are there teeth in there?

ACROSS THE casino floor Harry sees a man sweeping things into a dustpan. The man is dressed the same way Ed is dressed. Harry tries to make the man out. But discovers his eyes won't focus quite right.

Harry says, "We're way past swing, Ed."

Ed picks up his lighter, lights it, clicks it shut.

"Okey-dokey," Ed says.

Harry checks again and sees the collapsed husk of the cigarette pack, the old guy's last few drink tokes stacked neatly on the bar top. Over Ed's shoulder, toward the other end of the bar, the last woman at the bar, the last person at the bar, other than themselves—Harry sees her get up, smooth her dress with her hands, then sit back down.

"She's not showing," Harry says.

Ed does not answer. Ed, Harry sees, is looking off over at the guy with the dustpan.

Harry stands up.

He says, "I've got to get out of here."

Then Harry sits back down.

He rubs his eyes with the heel of his hand.

Ed says, "That's the trouble, isn't it, hooking the faces you forget up with the names you remember?"

Harry feels the old guy grip his elbow.

Harry sees Ed's wet eyes.

"Barkey," Ed says. "Barkey."

Harry stands up again. He looks over at the woman.

Ed says, "Most times I never forget a name at all."

Harry says, "She's not coming, Ed. Sue. It's definite that she's not."

"She always comes," Ed says.

Harry says, "It's way past between, I think."

"Sit down," the old guy says. "Let's get you fixed up."

Harry sees the woman stand, smooth her dress, then sit

back down again. From across the casino floor, he can hear the guy working the dustpan.

"Sit down," the old guy says. "I'll show you how to light your face on fire. In case you ever want to do it."

I Am Not So Old

THE SNOW had been falling all over and into itself. Everything was getting whiter and lighter and cleaner. Everything will be fine, Harry had thought on the way to the hospital, but now the sun was behind the clouds and was warming the snow to rain and everything that was white and light and clean was gray and heavy and muddy, and Harry was saying, "Another, please," and looking out the window at the two women who were crossing the street. He liked their little steps and their short coats and the way their arms folded hugging their breasts and when they turned the corner just in front of the bar he leaned forward, pressing his forehead against the glass to see if he could see more.

"Don't strain your neck, Harry," said the waitress, who was Celia.

Harry sat down and looked at his hands and saw Celia's hand with a beer appear. Then he saw Celia standing there, hovering. "How old are you, Celia?" Harry said.

"Thirty-four."

He looked up and saw her eyes and the red rouge slanting up under them.

"Is there something in my hair?" Celia said.

"No," said Harry. "How many beers have I had, Celia?" Harry said.

"This is your fifth," the waitress said.

When he had come in and it had been snowing, the beer was golden or amber or just like how they say it is on the TV, but now it was yellow and Harry wished there were more foam from it on top.

Die Blume they called the foam in Germany. *La fleur* they called the foam in France. The flower they called it. But Harry never got it with Celia because Celia was always trying to give Harry more beer and less foam. So Harry figured Celia did not know what the Germans and the French did.

"How old do you think those two were?" Harry said.

Celia winked and walked away.

"Hey, Celia!" Harry called.

Celia looked at him from across the bar.

"How old do you think I am, Celia?"

"My age?" the waitress said.

Harry didn't say anything but sat and drank.

"So how old are you, Harry?" the waitress said.

"Your age," Harry said.

He drank again and spread his hands flat on the table. Nicks and cuts marked his knuckles, and he started picking at a splinter in the heel of his hand.

"What're you doing here, anyway?" the waitress said.

"Just felt like having a beer," Harry said.

"I thought maybe you had something in mind," the waitress said. "Something else maybe."

"Nope," Harry said. "Nothing in mind."

"Are you all right?" the waitress said.

"Sure, I'm all right," Harry said.

Harry drank down his beer, lifting his glass high so Celia would know he was finished.

Celia said, "You want another one?"

Harry said he wanted another one, and the waitress brought over two beers, one for her and one for Harry. The beers came yellow and with no foam on them. Harry held up his glass and said, "Die Blume, la fleur, the flower." Harry said, "There is a street in Paris on the bank of this river, and the stores are so nice on this street, sort of like the Meadowood Mall, only not like it. They have all the newest things, whatever you could think of, all of them so different and selling different things. Hell, they sell everything. Not like here. And there's this stuff, which is like liver but not like any liver we have. Sort of soft, and tastes great, and sometimes it has these things in it. It tastes so good you think you could eat it forever, but you can't eat it forever because it tastes too good. And when the smells come out of the bakeries, even if it's just bread, you feel like you have to eat it. You can smell everything from far away. And you don't have to go back to your room and turn on the TV to watch some stupid thing or the news. You could just stay out and never do anything else. You could walk around and watch the light change until it got dark out. You could walk around in some new linen skirt you bought because that is what women wear there, and maybe a sweater sometimes because it's always nice out and never hot like here. You could walk. You could watch. You could just sit somewhere. Then when it starts getting dark and the white stone isn't so white anymore, you can go to where the lights are coming on. The lights there are always coming on."

"Oh, Harry," the waitress said.

"You are so pretty, Celia," Harry said.

He moved and knocked over his beer with his elbow. He leaned over the spilled beer and kissed her.

She said, "Oh, Harry."

Harry was trying to kiss her again. So she moved her head and let him kiss her neck. Harry thought he might be getting sick, but he only belched a little under his breath.

"What?" he said, without knowing he said what or what to or even that he was speaking or she was at all. There was only suddenly her neck and below that her breast and below that the stomach and below that was that—which was what he thought he wanted.

"Mmmm," he said, and tried to touch her breast.

The waitress said, "There are people." She said, "We aren't in Paris yet."

His fingers folded into fists and he stared straight into the spilled beer.

"You're just like her," he said.

"Her?" the waitress said.

"At the hospital," Harry said.

"Now?" the waitress said.

"Now," Harry said.

"You bastard," the waitress said.

She leaned away abruptly and hit Harry in the face and screamed, "You fucking bastard!"

Harry's eyes watered and some blood was on his lip. He didn't wipe it off but could taste it and it tasted like her and like the baby to him.

He said, "Okay."

Everything will be okay, he thought, getting up and getting into his coat. He could see that rain was falling now. There is still time, he thought. Anything is possible. I am not so old, he thought.

Great Basin

Either with the coyotes, it's that they're waiting to get rerun over by the Interstate eighteen-wheelers, or get fed off of on by the black-tailed magpies. With Clem and Irene, it's the day passing and the odds dropping from one-hundred-to-one to ten-to-one that one or more of the magpies will get theirs on the grill of an eighteen-wheeler as the birds turn sluggish in the desert sun. For Harry and his father, it is not knowing what not to watch between either the coyotes and the magpies, or Clem and Irene, or the cowboy boy and the Indian girl, who, even if you didn't look at or try to listen in on, it was still hard not to hear shrieking cowboy-and-Indian murder at each other from inside the foodstore section of Sierra Sid's Tank and Feed. It is Harry and his father trying to talk it over how much better it might have been to have picked a different stretch of desert to run out of gas in. Oh, it is all of it, all right—Clem and Irene, Harry and his father, the cowboy boy and the Indian girl, the coyotes, the magpies—if you thought much on it the way Harry had been given to think on it—beating the heat, killing the time.

Never mind that neither the Sierras nor Sid was anywhere in sight but only just Clem and Irene. Never mind that most of what Harry saw you were supposed to feed on in the foodstore section of Sierra Sid's Tank and Feed was past packaged due date by nearly about two years, six months, and eight days. Never mind especially why it was that there was no gas at Sierra Sid's Tank and Feed.

"Never you mind," Clem says, "it'll be along shortly."

Just try to fix it in your head first Irene, her being the lady, looking, then after, Clem, him being the man, looking through the WW I Army/Air issue field glasses down to the blur of black that is the Interstate, where, if you were Harry, you would after a time have taken the field glasses when they had been offered to see the magpie beaks pecking over coyote guts that seemed almost nearly like to bubble on the heated pavement.

"Oh, they like it that way," says Irene. "Them sons-of-bitches, they like their carrion hot."

"Don't you listen to her, young man," Clem says. "Those birds will take it how they can get it." Says Clem, "It's the word she likes to say, carry-on. Ask her why don't you what it means, hey? Go ahead and ask her!"

"You ask," Irene says, "and I'll tell you it means a dead thing that ain't no more. It's just a thing you can't even anymore remember how it was looking. Just a thing like the word of what it is—carry-on. And I'm telling you," Irene says, "them sons-of-bitches, they like their carry-on hot."

Harry's father, a giant to Harry's eyes of them all of the ones who are sitting out on the empty potato-salad buckets in the shade of the shed-roof porch, Harry's father says again, "Do they always fight like that?"

"Who's that you mean?" Clem says.

"The cowboy," Harry's father says. "And the girl."

"The Indian?" says Clem.

"The one who's fighting," Harry's father says.

"That'd be the Indian," Clem says.

"Course it'd be the Indian," says Irene. "Did you ever see it once when it wasn't an Indian?"

"No," Clem says. "No, Irene, I got to give it to you there. Never once did I see it when it wasn't an Indian."

"That boy," says Irene, "he does like his squaws."

Harry's father gets up from off of his potato-salad bucket, uncollapsing upward the bent segments of his long body, unbending up at first his neck, next his back, then his waist, and last his knees, all of him straightening to standing until Harry sees his father's head nearly touching clear up to the rotting rafters of the shed roof they are sitting under. His father lifts and drops his shoulders in circles, the stretchings and relaxings of his father's big-boned muscles seeming to Harry to roll boulderlike just beneath his father's T-shirt.

Clem and Irene, Harry is surprised to see, they never give a look. Clem and Irene are instead all four eyes out and down the Interstate, waiting on an Ameri-Mover with plates from Maine, a Seeley Bros. Kenworth hauling Arkansas hogs, or else Dick Cox's Peterbilt topped off with Nebraska wheat to make bread for the West, Clem and Irene waiting on each and every easterly-coming eighteen-wheeler to breathe a breath of life into the desert deadness of their day.

"What I mean," says Harry's father, Harry's father having himself another look-see into the foodstore part of Sierra Sid's Tank and Feed, "is why do you let them carry on like that?"

But Irene, she has got a hot one out on the horizon. She is goggle-eyed against the field glasses and is flapping her arms winglike for quiet. She is holding the field glasses out for Harry, and Harry can't help taking them to look, and with the eighteen-wheeler coming close at a grazing pace across the Interstate, eating up the miles of sage and alkali, growing from a formless yoke out of waves of heat, taking on truck shape and diesel roar, setting up in the desert floor a live vibration to tickle the soles of your feet on the porch, and with Clem and Irene raising the wagers on this eighteen-wheeler's passing from a nickel-to-a-hole-in-a-doughnut to a straight lead spender on whether or not the magpies would get this time theirs smack against the grill—it is hard for Harry with all of this to pitch in with his father in caring overmuch for what will or will not happen with what has been going on between the cowboy boy and the Indian girl in the foodstore section of Sierra Sid's Tank and Feed.

Maybe if his father had let Harry watch what was going on inside the foodstore part, Harry might have maybe cared more, or else if his father would have boughten for him a cupcake, or a fruitpie, maybe a Ding Dong, or maybe even only just a Ho Ho—he'd eaten older ones before, Harry had told his father, and they were perfectly good, perfectly fine—but his father wasn't buying it, he wouldn't buy a thing in there, Harry's father had said, and he was serious. He meant business. Harry's father had used the kind of a voice that for Harry to touch a single wrapper meant for Harry to find himself kicked into the middle of next week, meant for Harry to have his head put through the wall, for Harry to be wearing his asshole for a collar.

No thank you, sir!

So for now Harry is on his feet with Clem and Irene, screaming as eighteen-wheels worth of Wisconsin cheddar blasts past to rerun over coyote carry-on, mashing fur into pavement, scattering feathers skyward but to the unluck of Irene without taking a single magpie casualty, leaving Irene the loser, Irene making the next logical move of chasing her bet by raising the stakes in lieu of the odds being lowered. Clem meanwhile is wild. He is giving Irene what he calls Love Smacks to her backside, open-handed splats on the fat of her cheek. Clem is biting the lead with his yellowing teeth to check the authenticity of the nickel Irene hands him over.

Harry sits back down when Irene sits back down. They are looking to the Interstate to see the magpies settle ash- or dustlike back to pecking pavement-heated innards. They are Harry and Irene both looking from atop their potato-salad buckets to Harry's father hovering near the door to the foodstore section of Sierra Sid's Tank and Feed.

Harry's father says, "Is it really his?"

"I expect it is," Irene says.

"How old is that boy?" says Harry's father.

"Old enough," Irene says, "to have pulled this stunt more than twice."

"He's older than you think," Clem says. Says Clem,

"Say, you want maybe to make a little wager as to how old that boy is?"

"No," Irene says to Clem, "he doesn't want to make a wager. Can't you see a wagering man when you see him?" To Harry's father, who Harry sees is swelling up inside his T-shirt—his father's chest, his father's shoulders, his father's arms linked up with the kind of fists Harry knows you'd be better off on the right side of come some head-bender of a Saturday night—to Harry's father Irene says, "What the boy's trouble is, mister, is he hasn't got the good sense God gave a fencepost."

"Now, Irene," Clem says, "if you tell it right, you'll leave God and fenceposts out of this. What you ought to mean the trouble is with that one is he never wears his raincoat."

"It's what I said," says Irene, "in so many words. You never saw a fencepost getting into the kind of a mess you see in there, did you?"

"No," Clem says, "no, Irene. I never saw a fencepost doing much other than being just a fencepost. But I never saw either the fencepost yet that had much choice in what it was or what it wasn't."

Harry's father, Harry sees him looking back out on the humming heat, the high-ceilinged dome of mountain desert, a blank face of pale blue sky watching over the rounded shoulders of treeless ridges, the cracked bottoms of water-starved valleys. Harry sees his father wipe the sweat and grime from the canyon creases marked broad across his forehead, his father's cheek twitching at the clicking of cicadas. Harry's father says, "So how much longer on that gas truck?" and Clem, Harry sees him put his watch up near his ear, sees him gauge the sunlight with his thumb.

Says Clem, "Shortly."

Says Irene, Irene not uncollapsing upward so much to Harry's mind as she is bulging slightly higher from off her potato-salad bucket, a caterpillar, say, uncocooning before its rightful butterfly time, says Irene, bulging up, "Say, I think I'm going to get me a fruitpie."

"Fruitpie?" says Clem. "I wouldn't mind me a piece of that fruitpie, come to mention it."

To Harry, Irene says, "Would you like a piece? Would you eat a piece of fruitpie?"

Fruitpie! Who wouldn't kill for a piece of lemon? Or, no, not lemon, but cherry! Cherry? How about berry? Blueberry! And a Dr Pepper! No, no, it's not blueberry, it's lemon, lemon-flavored fruitpie Harry lives for.

But his father is so big! and there is no more fruitpie on his father's lips now than there was the hours ago when Harry and his father had to hike the last bit of desert to reach with gas can in hand the gasless pumps of Sierra Sid's Tank and Feed. There is no more fruitpie now than when Harry's father first stiffened up to hear how Clem and Irene had stood in the shade of the shed-roof porch, neither ever thinking to drive on out to pick them up, but only just watching Harry's father and Harry coming cotton-mouthed and sun-stroked through the WW I Army/Air issue field glasses. Never either, of course, was there other than no more fruitpie on his father's lips since his father had asked how it could anyway be that Clem and Irene let a man or a boy talk to a lady that way, Indian or not. Not even for love, not even for Irene's giving the reason of love to blame in the case of the cowboy boy and the Indian girl could there get to be any more fruitpie on Harry's father's lips, not even with Irene saying to Harry's father, "There are two things, mister, none of us has got one iota of control over—and one of them is love. The boy is in love. He gets in love a lot. He can't help himself." Says Irene, "I'm telling you the truth, mister. You haven't lost that pinched look from off your face since first we spotted you. You ran out of gas. You ain't unique. Now why not don't we all just have us a nice piece of this perfectly fine fruitpie while we wait on the gas truck to come? Clem says it'll be along shortly, and I'm sure it will be. I'm sure he's right by saying that much."

It is amazing, Harry is amazed, there is no other word for it, how Irene can't see for looking that not only is there no more fruitpie on his father's lips than when first they got here, but that there is getting to be even less fruitpie, that there is no fruitpie on his father's lips or anywhere else on his giant face—not on the eyebrow arch of his sunburned scar, not on the double bump of his twice-broken nose, nor the open pores of his sweat-leathery cheeks, nor not on any other part of the hard-lined face Harry's father has used and abused to always each and every single last time get exactly what he wants is there a smidgen of a hint of his altering off from what he has laid down as the law—nowhere, anywhere is there a Yes to fruitpie, lemon, cherry, berry, blueberry, or even a lively, sweetly carbonated sip of Dr Pepper, period.

Irene, though, still she never sees it, not the way Harry sees it, so Harry's father, he has to say it in an out-loud word, says the word his face, his arms, his chest, legs, and shoulders, the all of him that is so big and to Harry says it better, says the word, says, "No."

"No," Harry's father says, and, "No," is the echo of the Indian girl from inside the foodstore section. There is No from the Indian girl, and a something other than either the Indian girl or the cowboy boy coming from inside, comes a sound neither human nor animal either, what Harry hears as an inanimate, plastic pulling out, an umbilical ripping off of the phone from the wall, a crash and a plaintive single ding that Harry knows without a doubt is the phone thrown at the fruitpie display rack.

Irene, she is all undulating hips and quivering elbows in what Harry takes to be her quickest caterpillar crawl for the door to the foodstore section. Harry's father, Harry sees, he is moving the other way for the pay phone on the far end of the shed-roof porch. He is clawing in his pockets for quarters. Harry sees his father drop a quarter in the pay phone, sees his father hearing the line gone dead. And Clem, Harry sees him leaning into the field glasses, pulling for the magpies, slapping the hand railing as an entire convoy of eighteen-wheelers is born out on the eastern horizon.

Harry himself is glued to his potato-salad bucket as his father's footsteps boom back closer on the porch boards. Not for the more money Clem might be winning would Harry want to be Clem with the way Harry's father is eyeballing him. Not for even more money than that would Harry want to be the cowboy boy, who if either Clem or Irene cared to make a wager on it, Harry could tell them they would soon be meeting in the middle of next week, the boy's head punched through the plaster and sheetrock, the boy wearing a tight-buttoned fringe of rubberized rectum around his pencil-thin neck. Harry is not even sure if he would want to be Harry, wishes maybe he could be aboard the receding diesel roar and shrinking speck of truck that is the first of the three eighteen-wheelers disappearing down the Interstate. Harry wishes maybe he could be the magpies feasting in the wheel ruts of fur and guts, maybe even the coyote himself, dead and gone and never needing anymore to worry about where not to look for what you didn't want to happen next.

It is, Harry figures God to thank, Irene that happens next. It is Irene Harry hears calling out over the cemetery quiet coming now from inside the foodstore section. It is Harry's father not stopping Harry this time from going in with him to see the place where Irene is down on the floor, holding the cowboy boy propped against the steel door to the foodstore storeroom. Irene is stroking the boy's hair back off from where his hat had pressed it down. She is cooing to the boy, sugar-voiced, honey-tongued, sweet-talking the cowboy boy. Harry listens, can't help himself from looking to see how nearly Harry's age the boy after all seems to be. "There, there," Irene is saying. "There, there," she says, but the cowboy boy is not hearing. The cowboy boy, Harry sees, Harry sees his father seeing, is not hearing or seeing or feeling anything except for his own leg, his very own leg attached to his very own self, the cowboy boy not being able to take his eyes off from his very own self bleeding bad from a piece of broken-off metal he has got himself stuck arrowlike into his blue jeans.

"Umbrella," Irene says. "I've told him he'd get it sooner or later, romeoing around the reservation the way he does. Either from the girl's family or from the girl herself, sure bet, I've told him, he'd get it sooner or later."

"Sooner or later," Harry's father says, and Harry can see by the way of his father's saying that his father means the gas truck, when exactly the gas truck would be coming to get them from out of where they were.

Says Irene, turning loose the cowboy boy, the boy by now bone-white and speechless, says Irene, turning loose, "Will you watch after him, mister, while I run and see if Clem's got a key?" Irene says, "The girl's got the rest of that umbrella with her there in the storeroom. She says she knows how to use it on herself. She says she'll go ahead and use it on herself and get rid of what the boy gave her if he won't own up to what's his."

Harry's father puts his ear against the steel door to hear what he can from what is on the other side. Harry watches his father and knows by the firming up of his father's features that there would be a better chance of raising the re-run-over coyote from up off the Interstate pavement than there is for Harry's father to do anything like watching after. Harry sees there is growing in his father instead the better chance he might use the boy's hatless head as a battering ram to skip the key and knock the steel door down with.

Irene, Harry sees, she is gathering up the fruitpies on her way out to Clem. Fistfuls of phone-smashed fruitpies, she is gathering, torn bags of broken crusts and oozing goo— yellow, red, purple, and blue—slip-fingery textures of shining colors Harry has never before seen on either the dead or the live side of life.

Clem, coming in before Irene makes it out, Clem says, "What's this? Holy mackerel, Irene!" Clem says. "What'd you go and do to those fruitpies?"

"Carry-on," Irene says. "Fruitpie carry-on."

Says Harry's father, "Fruitpies? Fruitpies!" Harry's father says. "What'd this boy do to the telephone, is what I want to know! What about the girl? What I want to know is what exactly are you people doing here?"

Clem, thinking it over what it is he and Irene are doing, Clem says, "I suppose we're providing a service, is what we're doing."

"Service?" says Harry's father.

"Gas," Clem says.

"And food," Irene says.

"Like the sign says," says Clem. "Sierra Sid's Tank and Feed." Says Clem, "That was my idea, the sign was."

Says Harry's father, Harry's father stepping over the cowboy boy to get to close enough to where Clem will be sure to hear him, Harry's father says, "But the Sierras, Clem, they aren't here. This is the desert, Clem. You aren't Sid, Clem. Neither is Irene. Irene," says Harry's father, "are you Sid?"

"No, sir," Irene says. "I'm not Sid."

"Harry," says Harry's father, "are you Sid?"

"No, sir," Harry says. "I'm not Sid."

"Clem," says Harry's father, "Clem," Harry's father says, "fill her up for me, why don't you?"

"Fill her up?" says Clem.

"The can," Harry's father says. "Can you fill up the gas can for me?"

"You know I can't do that," Clem says.

"But you said you had gas, Clem. You said you provided a service," Harry's father says.

"I said we're out for now," Clem says.

Harry's father, he claps his hands, and, "Damn!" Harry's father says. "When can we expect the gas truck? You, Harry," says Harry's father. "When can we expect that gas truck?"

Says Harry, "Shortly?"

"That's right!" says Harry's father. "And how long has it been?" he says.

"A couple of hours," Harry says.

"Now, wait a minute," Irene says. "Clem can't help it, mister, when the gas truck comes or not. He just only knows what he knows, what he got told, what happens mostly around here. And I told you," says Irene, "that we got food. We got fruitpies."

Clem, sucking blue from off his fingers, Clem says, "We even got potato salad, usually."

Irene, she takes ahold of Clem at the elbow and Clem gives to Irene one of his Love Smacks on her backside. Says Irene, "Clem, he likes his potato salad."

"It's because of my teeth," Clem says, and Clem, he peels back his upper lip, indicating to them all there his sugar-rotted incisors.

Harry's father, Harry sees him take his first step back, his first step down. Harry sees some of the color leave his father's sunburned scar, thinks he sees the craters of sweat-leathery pores close up some on his father's cheek. Harry even thinks he sees his father deflating in his T-shirt—his father's shoulders, his chest, his arms, his father's fists unfolding into fingers.

His father says, "What?"

"My teeth," Clem says.

"Your what?" says Harry's father.

"My teeth," Clem says.

"He likes his potato salad," Irene says, "on account of his teeth being yellow."

Says Clem, "It reminds me, Irene, you owe me a dime, a quarter, and a fifty-cent piece."

"Convoy?" says Irene.

"Yes, ma'am," Clem says. "Say," Clem says, "what is it with our cowboy here, anyway?"

"Umbrella," Irene says.

"Damn," Clem says, "I never thought we should have bought those umbrellas. Well," Clem says, "did you give him some merthooliate?"

"Merthooliate?" says Harry's father. "What about the girl? What about the girl in there?"

"The girl's in there?" says Clem.

"It's what I was meaning to ask you," Irene says. "Before we got ourselves side-barred here. I was going to ask you about the key."

Clem, he gets thoughtful, and it is easy for even Harry to see that there is no key in any of Clem's pockets, and that there is no key on the peg Clem checks to make sure the Indian girl has already got it off of from. There is no key anywhere, Harry sees, to get to where the Indian girl has got herself.

Says Clem, "Girl? Girl, you give us out that key!"

But the Indian girl does not give them out the key. She does not answer. Clem asks again, allowing to them all on the outside as how the girl has got enough food to live off of in there for only God could say how long a time. Irene, she puts her ear to the steel door there next to Clem. Harry sees her grip tighten up on Clem's elbow.

"Quiet," Irene says. "Quiet, please."

Harry watches Irene listen, tries hearing what he figures Irene must be hoping to hear coming from the Indian girl's side of the storeroom door. Harry hears at first only just the under-sounds, the tickings and crackings of heated things cooling, wood, and metal things, plastics—the cash register, wall studs, and wheel rims—contracting, relaxing. Harry looks to Clem and then again to Irene, and then to his father listening to hear nothing but the growing sound of silence coming from the other side.

Harry's father, he opens his mouth up to speak. Clem, Irene, and Harry, the umbrella-stuck cowboy boy leaning against the steel door, they all look to Harry's father to learn what it is he has to say. But Harry's father is dumb-struck. He has nothing to say. Harry sees his father finding absolutely nothing that is finally right to say to any of what has happened to any of them who are gathered together there in the foodstore section of Sierra Sid's Tank and Feed. Harry's father lifts the callused hams of his unfisted hands from up off his sides. Harry sees his father's hands fall back down to where they were.

Harry's father is out the door, where Harry follows to see his father need to stretch to reach up to the rotting rafters of the shed-roof porch. Harry sees his father holding on, sees his father feeling something not quite solid. Harry's father is looking to Harry to be almost smooth-faced now, his father showing an almost baby-faced gaze out to the heat-faded blue, the lip-blistering shimmer of the endless desert. Harry's father turns loose the rotting rafter, col-lapsing himself downward, rebending up the straightened segments of his long body, first his knees, then his waist, next his back, last his neck, reversing himself, re-cocooning himself until all of him is sitting on the empty potato-salad bucket the same as all the rest had sat. Harry sees his father staring at his feet, Harry's father seeming to Harry to be trying to figure the porch-board vibrations sent up from across the desert floor by the last of the eighteen-wheelers that Clem and Irene still inside have missed seeing to bet on.

But there are other eighteen-wheelers for Clem and Irene. And there gets to be fruitpie for Harry. There gets to be Dr Pepper. There gets to be any sweet thing Irene has got to offer from out of in the foodstore section of Sierra Sid's Tank and Feed. Never mind the No that had been on Harry's father's face. Never mind the middle of next week, your head through the wall, what you might be wearing for a collar. Never mind especially how fast the remains of the day have passed without the gas truck ever coming.

Just fix it in your head first Irene, her being the lady, ending up by staying behind to mind the foodstore section of Sierra Sid's Tank and Feed, and then Clem, him being the man, finally loading up at last the cowboy boy to go to town for a doctor and a locksmith to fetch out and see what about the Indian girl on the other side of the store-room door.

"Don't you worry, mister," Irene says to Harry's father. "Clem'll be back shortly."

But Harry's father does not hear. Not since his last long-legged kick at the unbudging steel of the storeroom door has Harry's father moved to hear or to see any of what has gone on around him. Harry's father has sat rigor-mortis stiff on his potato-salad bucket through the day's waning and far beyond its noontime maturation, hours past the pungent scent of sweating sage, the early arousal of the first crickets sounding off the decline into night, the bleeding streaks of dying light touched off from the withered skin of sun now sunk beneath the western desert mountains. Harry's father has shown no sign of feeling even the sudden drop by tens of degrees the air they have all been made to suffer in, no sign of seeing how the coyote carrion has gone too cool for the magpies to care about, leaving what is left alone. Harry's father has not to Harry's knowing registered either the evening out of the betting between Clem and Irene, Clem losing the last bad bet on a single magpie death, all of his wins on the narrow escapes by the life-saving flights of the black-tailed birds wiped out on the barreling grill of a Global Transport eighteen-wheeler, Irene beating the way she said a person always eventually does, the lowest odds with the highest stakes.

Harry sees his father sitting on an empty potato-salad bucket. Harry sees the darkness soften the last hard lines of his father's face. Harry watches his father watching the red eyes of Clem's taillights winking out of sight. Harry's father, he gets up from off of his potato-salad bucket, not unfolding so much to Harry's eye now as he is just getting up, a man getting up from where he was sitting down. Harry's father says, "I'll meet him back at the car. I'm going back to the car," he says. To Harry, Harry's father says, he asks, "Do you want to come with me?"

And Harry, warm there near Irene on the shed-roof porch, his belly full of fruitpie and Dr Pepper, full of all the sweet things Irene has given to him, Harry says to his father, "No. No," he says, "no, I think I'll wait here."

"All right," his father says. His father says, "Okay. Sure. You wait here. I'll be back. You just wait here for me," says Harry's father, and Harry's father is gone into the night, his father's footsteps sounding somehow delicate, eggshells breaking in the desert, his father's back shrinking into folds of mountain shadow.

Further off, toward where the horizon during the hot part of the day once was, Harry sees how you can see the glare, the blinding shine of headlights from the eighteen-wheelers forever coming on from out of the dark, sees how you can feel it in your seat the low rumble and the still air shake with the unrelenting weight of cargo carried west to them from the rest of the world—and how, much closer, down near the interstate, you can hear the coyotes coming singing in the evening, a mourning, a mournful serenade, a lover's song sung over the ears of the dead.

Something New

"THINK I'LL GET some new gloves," Harry says.

"Pardon me?" she says.

Harry sees her lean back from the eggs. He sees her dig her fingers into the low part of her back, sees how fat she has gotten off of all the ice cream she says she has to eat.

"Looks cold," he says. "I said I could sure use some new work gloves for this cold."

"New gloves?" she says.

"Work gloves," he says. "My hands are splitting."

Harry moves behind her. He sees the beads of grease roll around and disappear on the Teflon. He touches her belly and tries to feel what's going on inside. He likes feeling for it. But this morning Harry cannot feel it kick.

She says, "Didn't you just get some new gloves?"

"A while back," Harry says. "A month maybe. I don't know."

"Can't you wait on new ones?" she says.

"Wait?"

"I mean, maybe the weather will change."

"Oh," he says. "I see. Maybe. Yeah, I guess I could wait for the weather to change."

Harry breaks off a piece of bacon and eats it. He hefts his belly in his hands. He has gotten fat, too. Harry has gotten fat to where his tool-belt buckle is hidden under his overhang of belly.

He says, "They're shot to hell, the gloves are."

She says, "Well, it seems to me like you just got some new gloves. Seems like you're always getting new ones."

Harry takes a knife out of the drawer and sits to butter the toast. He does not use the jam because the jam is saved for her to use on her ice cream. Harry wonders if even after she has had the thing she will keep on eating ice cream and never not be fat.

"I was thinking of suspenders, too," he says.

Harry sucks his belly in to where he can see his belt, and then he lets his belly out. Harry thinks how she has shown him the way her fat has grown so she can hold her ice-cream bowl on her belly without the use of her hands.

He says, "What do you think of suspenders?"

"I think you don't need suspenders," she says.

Harry says, "Maybe I don't need suspenders. But I'll tell you what—it's been a long time since I got new gloves. It's been a long time since I've gotten a new anything at all. Can you remember me getting anything new?"

"No," she says. "I can't remember you getting anything new. So get your goddamn gloves," she says. "You said you needed new gloves—so get your new gloves."

"I said my hands are splitting," he says. "I said it looks cold today, is what I said."

"It is cold today," she says. "I know it's cold."

He says, "Cold enough for new gloves, anyway. Wouldn't you say so?"

"I said it was," she says. "I said it was cold today. So you better go and get yourself your brand-new gloves."

Harry refolds the paper to the sports and pours himself another cup. She brings his plate. She sits across from him and takes the crossword-puzzle page.

"How about those classes?" he says.

"What classes?" she says.

"Oh, you know," he says. "Those exercise classes we signed you up in."

"What about them?" she says.

"Are you going?"

"I go sometimes," she says.

Harry pushes his toast through the yellowish mess and watches her fold the paper in half and in half again. She begins to fill in the blanks. Harry sees her tap the pencil when she gets stuck.

"It's not much," he says. "New gloves. New gloves aren't asking too much."

"No," she says. "They aren't much."

"I really need them," he says.

"Then get them," she says.

"I could get frostbite," he says. "You know Tom? From work? Tom got frostbite once. You wouldn't want me to get frostbit, would you?"

"Hey, listen, I'm trying to do this," she says.

Harry says, "Well, these eggs are good."

She says, "I'm glad you think so. And I'm glad you're getting your new gloves, too."

Harry gets up and goes over to the refrigerator. He brings

back to the table a jar of her jam. He sticks his knife into the jam. But he does not use any. He sees her scratching out the parts she can't answer. He screws the lid back on the jar.

Harry says, "How much ice cream do you figure you eat in a day?"

She looks up at him. Then she looks back down. Harry sees her writing something at the bottom of the page. He runs a finger through the smear on his plate. He can hear her pressing harder on her pencil. He shifts his plate on the table so she will know that he is finished.

"No," he says. "I mean it. I'm just curious. I was just wondering about how much."

She gets up to take his plate. Harry watches the way the meaty part of her arm hangs and wobbles as she reaches. He starts to reach to see if he can feel anything kicking around in there. But then he thinks he'd better not.

He says, "I can always just pick up a pair of cheap ones."

"Sure," she says. "You can get the cheap ones."

"Of course, they don't last you as long," he says.

"So get the good ones," she says.

"It's just that they last," Harry says. "The good kind."

"Get them," she says. "Get the good kind if you want."

He says, "Do you think I should?"

"I do," she says.

"I need them," he says. "Some good ones probably."

He goes to fetch his coat from off the counter. He looks to see what she has written down under the puzzle. He puts his coat on and goes over to the door.

Harry says, "How're you fixed for ice cream? Can I bring you back some ice cream?"

"No," she says. "I don't need any ice cream."

"Because I can get it," Harry says.

"I'm fine," she says.

"So long as you're sure," Harry says.

He opens the door. He feels the rush of air on his face. His pickup gleams in the winter sun. He gives a little whistle, claps his hands together, and shuts the door.

Willows

I T WAS EASY, really, the business with the willows. It was
the colonel who wanted the willows clipped. They'd all
seen him. Each fall season they had all seen the old man
burn and spray and hack at the stand of willows, which
would always grow back thick along the ditch bank over
the course of the following summer when the water ran
fast in a flowing gush the color of mud. From the downside
edge of the grassy slope the colonel kept mowed close to
the ground behind his big-windowed house, you could see
each season the sunlit glint of steel that marked the slashing
motion of the old man's spit-shined machete. Thrashings,
you could see, animals in the underbrush. But never the
colonel himself clear and complete. Songs, and whistlings,
you could hear, signs, and you could see the boys spying
from the span of bridge passing over the dried-up ditch,
Harry and Tom among them, stretching their necks to get
a glimpse, listening close to pick up the best of the colonel's
pirate curses, the boys keeping their noses covered against

the black clouds of green willow smoke and the windswept spray of poison.

There were rumors. People said the old man used a rifle—that he shot squirrels and rockchucks and rabbits. And cats, they said he shot, though mostly spraying males nobody much blamed him for. But the fathers winced at mongrels, then claimed the old man was crossing the line at purebreds, and some of the mothers wondered about the child who cried of nearly being missed by one of the colonel's whining bullets. No bird sang or shat upon the colonel's property. He fed rice to the birds to watch their stomachs explode. When Harry himself was younger, he used to believe the old man existed only as an apparition, a nighttime traveler hanging in the billowed forms of curtains, waiting at the window to claim the first sleeping child to open his eyes and get caught looking where he ought not to have ever looked.

The truth was—what you could count on and know for certain—was that only once for some weeks in the willow-cutting season of the year did the old man appear from out of his big-windowed house, and yearly were Tom and Harry there to witness his workings. So it was easy, really, if you could come in those years to see the old man as any other man made out of the aging flesh and blood he really was, stripped of story, minus the mask of magic slipping slowly away from his unseen face as the years passed and the boys came to see themselves as growing wiser with the seasons—was easy, really, if you saw Harry as one of those boys, the way the job of clipping the colonel's willows was handed on down to him.

What was harder was the boy. You could call him Lester,

or Maurice, or Sydney. Any name to practice a lisping tongue thrust too long and held too soft on the front of the teeth a person rarely saw on him in either speech or laughter. *Lethter, Maurithe. Thydney*, you could call him. You could know him by his lisp and by his hands placed resting lightly on his hips, thumbs pointed forward after the girlish fashion that he had. *Oh, Lethter!* you might have heard. *Thay, Thydney!* Harry remembered. But what Harry thought of even more than a name, when he remembered the boy, was paper doilies, say, lacy, delicate things, things like silken sheets and shade, white skin and cool breezes, lips, kisses, slim-waisted ladies showing slips from dresses, and shaved legs, and an arm, too, Harry would think of, the boy's arm, twisted, pushed up and turned behind his back in the grade-school way, his face pressed into the playground sand and a crowd surrounding around Jackie Price, who early on had made it his job to pound the boy into saying the names they gave him.

But the boy never said the names. Not for Jackie Price, not for any of the other boys who stood shouting there behind him—Harry and Tom included. Because it was true that Harry and Tom were no different from any other person who ever saw the chance to bully the things he was most afraid of. Harry and Tom had helped to paint the boy's face with lipstick and rouge, helped to hold the boy still while waiting for the glue-lined wig to dry on his head. It was Harry who taught the other boys what in the world a hermaphrodite was, and it was Tom who supplied the circus freak pictures. But it was Jackie Price who pushed the game further by trying to make the boy to drop his pants and show them whether or not it was true. In every game and in every way it was Jackie Price that Harry remembered as being the one to take things with the boy to the point where Harry found himself, even before the willows, wishing to hear the shrilling of the teacher's whistle calling them off the playground.

But for all that Jackie Price had studied to come up with to do to the boy, the boy still never said the names, nor ever showed them the private parts of himself either. The boy kept instead more and more to himself through the years, and his eyes took on a fishflat blackness that always held its look no matter what they all thought he must have felt as they witnessed Jackie Price's weekly beatings.

Nobody told. Nobody told because, as Harry had said, there were none of them at the time afraid of the boy so much as they were of Jackie Price. It made sense to be afraid of Jackie Price. It made sense to be afraid until the season Harry took the job to cut the colonel's willows.

THEY WERE COMING floating down the ditch, Harry and Tom, in the summer when the colonel asked them. Against the sun in their eyes they could see the shape of the colonel hotfooting it down the grassy slope of his close-mowed lawn. It was Harry's idea from the beginning, Harry suggesting that he and Tom grab hold of the willows to wait and see what had brought the old man out before the ditch was drained and it was time for the blade. The old man wore a Panama hat, Harry had seen and remembered, and he carried not a rifle but a cane, and he dressed in a shade of black that hid his face in shadow. Harry turned and saw Tom staying back in the cover of the willows as the colonel's clawed hands clasped the bridge railing from where he addressed them, making the offer, to either one or the both of them together, of a hundred dollars cash to cut the willows down.

Harry could feel the tug of the summer's muddy water on his calves. He looked at Tom, and he looked at the shape of the colonel standing there above them, and then he tested the supple toughness of the willow in his hand and figured it was worth it, never seeing the sweat it would take to earn the hundred-dollar bill the old man had dangled off the bridge in front of Harry's nose. So Harry said he'd do the job and he turned the willow loose, and together he and Tom passed underneath the darkness of the bridge, hearing the colonel whistling in the summer sun from up above, singing, *We'll see you in the fall, Drake, we'll see you in the fall.*

IN THE FALL it was when Harry first heard the boy's voice from up on the trail. It was while sitting underneath the bridge where they had floated through not so long ago that Harry first heard the boy and knew by the leafy lilt and birdsong coming of his words exactly who it was. It was while scraping the aphids out from his ears and shaking the tiny spiders from his hair, mixing willow grease with the sweat on his face, bitching and moaning and figuring from what work he had done and what was left ahead that in Harry the colonel had bought himself a one-bill slave. But it was not the boy's voice, not the big-lipped lisping of the boy that Harry listened to on the high side of the willows, but the man's. Not in Harry's house, or in any of the houses of all his friends, had Harry ever heard a voice like the voice of that one man's. Cancer, Harry heard in the man's voice, quick-killing disease and back-alley danger, knives and fists and a tone pitched to straddle the border of what is recognizable as human. Harry could hear the voice speaking to the boy in a language that made the colonel's seasoned curses seem the callow work of a half-hearted actor. Harry listened, and listening he could know right off how it was that Jackie Price and his schoolyard beatings had never got the boy to come out from where he had hid himself, could know that neither the number nor the kind of years that Jackie Price had lived could match the hauntful rasp that Harry heard cursing the boy up there on the trail.

Harry began to follow the boy and the man for much the same reason and in much the same way as he had followed the colonel in the years preceding, keeping himself nearly side by side with the two up on the trail above him. He picked and hopped his way along, and was careful to miss the lingering pools of water and the sticks and twigs that would give him away. He stepped around the stones where the sun never shone and the water clung concealed in the slippery sponges of lichens and moss that had set him flat on his backside more than once in the past. He spotted out the loudest yellow-baked leaves fallen from off the cottonwoods. Harry bent his knees and held his breath whenever he came up near to where they walked, peering to get a clean glimpse of the man and boy through the wall of willow green that grew thick up there between them, straining his ears to hear what in the circles of his own life he had not.

But quiet as Harry was, the colonel had been quieter, the colonel who had come from behind on the silent tread-way of his close-cut lawn to show Harry the old man still had some words left in him to bump up the flesh on a young boy's arms, the colonel catching Harry two knuckles deep, digging willow grease and aphids from out of his nostrils as he leaned to listen to the boy and the man. Snot Fuck! the old man called Harry. Lily Shit! he called him. What did Harry mean by being such a Limp Dicked Ass Jacker? the colonel wanted to know. What kind of a Snoopy Bitch Gossip Queen had he hired here? the old man asked.

Harry spun to see the colonel then not as a shadowy shape against the light of the sun, and not as a cane-wielding, Panama-hatted elder statesman, either. What Harry saw was to his knowledge the first clear sighting of the colonel by any among the pack of boys that Harry ran with. He was there, the colonel, framed for Harry by the one-eyed window of the old man's house that loomed watchful in the upslope background. He was standing in a pair of sneakers and a jockstrap and a regulation set of aviator sunglasses that Harry could see himself reflected in. Harry saw himself in the aviator sunglasses hustling back to the bridge, where he had left the machete and the tree shears, explaining to the old man that, no sir, he, Harry, didn't personally himself think he was any of what the colonel had suggested he might be—Snot, Lily, Limp, or Other—but that he was only thinking he maybe knew that boy to talk to. Harry worked himself from a hustle to fairly running back to the bridge as if he believed the old man might have the rifle somehow stuck inside his

jockstrap, Harry keeping an eye out to watch as the colonel
came on slipping down the ditch bank in his slick-bottomed
sneakers. He hadn't paid Harry to talk, the old man was
saying—and he said he wasn't any impressed with the way
Harry had been working when he wasn't wanting to talk,
either.

The colonel took the machete and it wasn't technique
that Harry watched as the colonel fell to working—it was
the colonel's hair. Harry had never seen the kind of body
hair he saw the colonel sporting. It was silver and white
and it was everywhere where there was skin to grow it.
Arms, chest, shoulders, back, ass and legs and stomach,
hands, and maybe even palms and nails, thick and curling
and really no sort of hair at all, Harry thought, but fur. It
was animal fur, and they were animal sounds the colonel
made as he worked his way deeper into the willows, cleav-
ing the willows easy at the trunk, never retreating from
the retaliatory sting and slap of branches Harry himself
had ducked from on the little he had done. Grunts and
growlings and stuck-pig squealings shook the brush and
caused Harry to recount to himself the stories he had once
believed before the years had led him to his newfound
wisdom.

The old man emerged from the willows panting and
hacking up some yellow stuff from in his chest, and Harry
saw the colonel seemed to notice neither the willow grease
that matted his fur, nor the teeming life of unnamable
insects that his body had since become host to. Harry
watched as the colonel made himself a willow switch, saw
the colonel flick the switch through the air, whipping up
a cutting sound that seemed to please him, and then the

old man held the machete out to Harry and told him it was his turn.

Harry took the machete and felt the colonel's sweat on the leather handle and heard the cutting of the colonel's willow switch. Harry picked the smallest willow and swung a chop that hardly nicked the trunk. Harry raised the blade for another swing, but felt the colonel's clawlike hand grabbing at his wrist to hold him back. The old man's other hand held on to Harry's waist, and Harry could smell the stale-meat smell of the spit on the colonel's breath as he whispered now in Harry's ear to stay away and leave the man and boy alone. Just leave them be, the colonel whispered, let them do what they will do. Nearly every day, the colonel whispered, the man and boy passed down this ditch trail, since long before Harry had seen them today and before Jackie Price had made it his job to work the boy over—never mind how the colonel knew about that— since clear back to the time when the boy was small enough to ride astride the man's shoulders, the colonel had seen them coming. He could see it all, the colonel said, from the big-windowed view up in his house, and he was watching, and he was watching Harry until he finished with the willows—and maybe even after.

So Harry passed it on to Tom, the job of finding out about the boy and the man, and Tom followed the two for a time before seeing the place where they disappeared from the ditch trail and down into the tallest bitter brush at the bottom of the gully. Tom would squat, reporting what he had seen back to Harry, talking down to Harry from the ditch trail through the daily growing, stump-dotted space where once were the willows Harry had clipped and hacked. Tom told Harry that never once had there been any contact between the boy and the man, no pushing or shoving or hitting, but that what Tom had seen was the boy moving forward in prodless shocks of motion. The voice was the prod, Harry had said, along with all that the man's voice promised, and what was promised, Harry knew, must be what went on between the two at the bottom of the gully.

Tom kept following and Harry kept waiting underneath the bridge to listen, and it got to where he thought he might be looking forward to hearing the man's voice, got to where, when the boy's lilting lisp came on ahead of the man, Harry could hear the run of bubbles popping in his stomach at the idea that he might one day ignore the sticks and twigs and slippery mosses and come on up the ditch bank to give himself away on purpose.

And it wasn't, as Harry remembered it, the fear of giving himself away that kept him under the bridge, so much as it was the fear of the colonel's watching.

AFTERNOONS, Harry spent with one eye checking always upslope for signs of moving life behind the giant glass of the old man's watching window, listening in the lapses of his working through the birdless quiet for the colonel's footfall coming daily on the yellowing pad of grass. Nights, Harry saw the colonel in his dreams, Harry carrying with him into sleep the thoughts and scenes the old man had put into Harry's head during the dusking hours when he worked. Harry would hear the colonel speaking from the spot where Harry had looked to see no living soul not three swings previous. Harry would see the old man standing even in the cold and rain of the later weeks wearing nothing save his fur to warm him. The old man would hiss and spit and Harry would wish for just one time for there to be a witness other than himself to the manner of the old man's appearance and the strangeness of his words. The colonel, Harry learned, had always known about the rumors flown around him. The cats, the old man knew about, the dogs, the children, and the birds it was said he shot at. The colonel neither confirmed nor denied the rumors but gave instead to Harry new things to think and dream, what the colonel called his military secrets, which he posed to Harry as questions. The colonel would crouch, prowling, eyebrows raised above the rim of his aviator sunglasses, asking Harry whether did he notice the concrete mowing strips, or the tin-sheet siding on his house? The colonel would slow his prowling, lower his voice so Harry had to come up close to listen, the old man asking did Harry care to guess the number of dry goods in the old man's cellar? had Harry thought yet why in the colonel's yard you would never see a tree? And then the old man asked the question no one had ever thought to ask, wondering had Harry considered this—considered why in God's world the colonel would ever want the willows cut down in the first place?

Harry never guessed and he never got an answer, and each day he would watch the colonel to make sure it was two feet and steps the old man had to take to get back to the top of the slope and the big-windowed house from where he sat and watched. Harry waited, watching, listening—the colonel on the one side of the ditch, the boy and man there on the other—and the leaves turned from green to red then gold and dying amber and the insects fell away in a single night's freeze and each day passed the same as the last with Harry working his slave-wages way through the willows that bent and swayed in the late autumn wind even as he cut them, hacking and clipping and chopping the living willows at the ground, the stacked and severed branches stiffening in mounds, and what was once the thick and thriving wall between Harry and the man and boy now became a void, a row of tough and bloodless stumps.

IT HAPPENED near the end, near the time when Harry had nearly cleared the willows completely, that Tom reported back to Harry that Jackie Price was following now, that Jackie Price had gone where Tom could never get himself to go, trailing the man and boy to the bottom of the gully. It happened near the end, too, that Jackie Price began finally to get the boy to say the names they gave him. Without a single arm twisting, no head banging or punching or any other kind of schoolyard drubbing—you could see the boy's eyes light up from the fishflat blackness they had all become accustomed to, and he would set his hands to resting slimly on his hips to do a mincing little two-step, saying, *Thydney, boys, I'm Thydney, look at me, Maurithe*! And the boy showed himself to those who stood behind Jackie Price, and even still with knowing what they knew, Harry and Tom did not step out of line but looked on with all the rest. It was a looking without seeing, as Harry recalled it, Harry recalling not wanting anymore to be a part of whatever it was that Jackie Price had learned to use to make the boy come out, Harry not wanting to see any of the things that had been made to be shown.

Whatever it was that Jackie Price had learned to use it was not to last, as they had all seen in less than one week's time the boy go back to what he was, then on to something worse that even Jackie Price could see and had no more nerve to touch. And it was not only Jackie Price who had changed his bullying ways but the man as well, whom Tom reported now as seeming to follow the boy rather than prod him down the trail. It was the boy Harry had heard from beneath the bridge, the boy ceasing with his lisping —and the man, whose voice had helped keep Harry all this time in the darkness where he was, leaving off in turn. It was the colonel, though, who seemed somehow to Harry to make the whole thing final, coming around now to burn and brush over the countless willow stumps, dipping to paint and rigging the pump and wand to spray from his bucketful of poison, whistling and singing to Harry now that *It's coming to a head, Drake, it's coming to a head.*

So that Harry was not much surprised when he heard the shots that came up from the gully. Six shots Harry counted but never told of hearing. Neither, when the time came, did Harry admit to seeing Tom, who had met Harry running down the ditch trail from where the shots had sounded. Tom had grabbed at Harry's arm, pushed at his back, trying to get Harry to run with him for home. But Harry would see what he had heard and know what he had guessed at, and so he had gone and he had seen them, seen all three—Jackie Price, the boy, and the man stretched dead in the clearing near the bitter brush at the bottom of the gully. Harry had seen the boy standing naked with the gun and with the man that he had shot laid out there at his feet. Harry had seen Jackie Price, his face paste-white with fear, stumbling and lunging up the gully, the only one among them to testify against the boy in court, Jackie Price claiming those six shots were not in self-defense, that the boy had made the man to kneel before him and beg his pardon before ever he pulled the trigger.

THERE WAS not much surprise in any of it, really, Harry figuring that these things have been happening since past when any single person could remember or even guess. They were the things that you could think on till you could see that you would never see the end and it was too late to go back to the start. Ten, fifteen, twenty years further in your life, you could know in it all no more or less than when you stood with both feet squarely in the middle. You could know that the man was dead and buried, that the boy had been sent and was gone to someplace far away. You could know that Tom and Harry had, in the winter of that year, lost their fear of Jackie Price and pushed him face first onto the frozen ditchwater to trip and knock his teeth out. You could know that the colonel had finally died and the willows had grown back along the ditch bank with nobody yet to try again to cut them.

And if you were Harry, you would often remember and think of the colonel in the way that he was when last you had seen him, Harry sometimes thinking that maybe the colonel had known it all from his big-windowed house, where he had sat the years and watched, the colonel pointing his finger at Harry and Tom and the bloodied gums of

Jackie Price, the old man laughing, bending at his silver-furred waist, lowering his voice then and speaking through his spitting to them all, the colonel seeming to Harry to be like nothing else but the hissing in the willows next to where you walk, whispering to you in your listening ear the things best left kept secret.

The Route

HARRY PULLED on the rope, testing the weight of the papers on the sled. They were the Sunday papers. Underneath the plastic coverings where the snowflakes fell and melted he could see the color pages of the comics. Harry saw the way the snow was already filling in the tracks left by his car.

Harry's son said, "You didn't have to meet me, you know."

Harry watched the snow falling straight through the streetlight. He could remember himself on a bike on Sundays, using the front-and-back-type canvas sacks to deliver the papers, and how the weight of the papers in the back made the canvas cut into his neck and throat, choked him as he got rid of the papers in the front. Harry felt how light the papers felt on the sled. "How's your mother?" Harry said.

"Oh, you know," said the boy. "Fat."

Harry listened to his son tip the bottle the boy kept hidden in the cinder-block wall. His son, Harry guessed, was either eleven or twelve. Harry could smell the clean smell of hard alcohol.

"Christ," the boy said, "I hate collecting. I hate going into old people's houses. It always stinks like old people. They always make you come into their stinking houses, and then they can never find their money. Except for Mrs. Segerstrom, I think I'd pay somebody to collect for me. I don't give a shit about Disneyland."

Harry looked away from his son and across the street to where the word FUCK was spray-painted on the street-light pole. He breathed in through his nose and felt the cold stick in his nostrils. Aside from his tire tracks, the snow was smooth. All the windows in the houses, Harry saw, were dark.

Harry's son said, "One time I saw a different man coming from Mrs. Segerstrom's."

Harry saw how the snow hit him at the shins, his son nearly at the knees. He saw the snow begin to stick instead of melt on the plastic covering the papers. Harry heard the bottle being lifted again.

"Really," said the boy, "I've done it in deeper snow than this."

"Does your mother know you drink?" said Harry.

The boy brushed the snow from off the papers.

The boy said, "What's your favorite comic strip?"

Harry touched his finger to the bump on his nose at the same place he saw it on his son's nose. He saw the red in his son's cheeks. Harry ran his hand against the stubble of his beard, watched his son's breath rise and mix with the falling snow.

"Mrs. Segerstrom tips," Harry's son said. "One time she gave me five bucks," he said. "One time I saw her nipples through the shirt she was wearing."

Harry lifted his feet from out of the snow, first one, then the other. He wiggled his toes inside his boots. Up and down the street Harry could see the way all the windows were still dark. It was the part of it he remembered he never much liked, making tracks in the snow when it was so smooth the way it was. Sometimes he thought it was almost better on the bike and having the weight of the papers in the back cut into your neck and throat than to make tracks like that.

The boy said, "But still I hate collecting. I hate to ever even see the people. Old fucks. Any of them, really. Fuck Disneyland," Harry's son said.

"What did you say about your mother?" Harry said.

"Fat," Harry's son said.

"Fat," Harry said.

"She eats grapefruit, hard-boiled eggs, and Oreos," the boy said.

The snow, Harry saw, was sticking again to the plastic covering the papers. The papers began to feel heavier to him on the sled. His feet, he thought, might be losing their feeling.

Nobody was up, Harry thought. Nobody knew.

Harry's son said, "You should have seen that guy, I mean the one coming out from Mrs. Segerstrom's. You should have seen his face when he saw me coming."

"Yeah?" said Harry. "You like collecting from her?"

"She's hot," Harry's son said.

Harry watched his son brush the snow from the plastic, take another swig from the bottle. He watched the face his son made and saw the snow stuck on top and circling around the sides of his son's stocking cap. He saw his son blink against the falling flakes, saw the red in his son's cheeks getting redder. Harry slid the sled back and forth.

"You're no angel," Harry said. "You stink."

The boy screwed the cap back on the bottle, put the bottle back in the cinder-block wall.

The boy said, "You don't have to help."

Harry began to walk up the street, pulling the sled behind. He did not look back to the footprints and to the sled tracks he knew he was leaving behind. He kept his eyes on the smooth snow ahead.

Harry said, "I'm not going to help."

"Then give me the rope," the boy said.

Harry stopped walking, put his finger to his lips.

"Listen," Harry said.

The boy stuck his neck out from his coat and narrowed his eyes, making as if to listen. Harry brushed the snow from off the newspapers. He picked up one of the newspapers, got a good grip on one of the corners. Harry threw the newspaper. The newspaper banged off the front door of somebody's house. Harry waited until he saw a light come on in one of the windows, then started again to pull the sled.

Harry's son said, "I don't hear anything."

"This route," Harry said, "was mine a long time before it was yours."

"You've never walked a step of this route," said the boy.

Up the street Harry could see the dark windows waiting. The snowflakes were melting on his cheeks. The Sunday newspapers felt to him like nothing.

"What is it you hate about this most?" Harry said.

"Collecting," the boy said. "I hate to even see the people. They can keep their fucking Disneyland."

Harry picked up another paper and banged it off the next door, and again he waited for the light to come on before moving to the next house.

Harry said, "But the sled is great, isn't it?"

The snow felt good the way Harry thought all good things must feel—the weight of it, the lightness of it. Harry listened, but could hardly hear the footsteps of his son.

"Sure," said the boy, "the sled is fine."

Harry stopped walking, turned to look at his son. Then he reached for another newspaper. Harry took aim through the falling snow. Then he lowered his arm and handed the newspaper to his son. Harry watched his son raise his arm to throw.

"Don't you hate it," Harry said, "when there's no snow and you're on your bike and you've thrown everything from up front and the weight chokes you from behind?"

"I guess," said the boy. "But not as much as collecting."

Harry watched his son throw, heard the newspaper strike the door, waited on the echo of the light.

A NOTE ABOUT THE AUTHOR

Sam Michel was graduated from the University of California at Berkeley, where his studies were concentrated in philosophy. He lives in Nevada and in Montana. *Under the Light* is his first book.

A NOTE ON THE TYPE

The text of this book was set in Sabon, a typeface designed by Jan Tschichold (1902–1974), the well-known German typographer.

Composed by Crane Typesetting Service, Inc., West Barnstable, Massachusetts. Printed and bound by The Haddon Craftsmen, Inc., Scranton, Pennsylvania.

Designed by Peter A. Andersen.